SHADOWS

ENDORSEMENTS

"Millions are living in the shadows and Travis inspires and intrigues in his wonderful work, *Shadows,* that also illuminates the path toward hope and healing."

—**Stephen Arterburn**, co-author of
Everyman's Battle and Founder of New Life Ministries

"In *Shadows*, Travis W. Inman gives readers a glimpse into the heart and mind of one good man ... with feet of clay. Using a kaleidoscope of emotion, Inman sheds light on the dark secrets that hide deep inside all of us, a stark reminder that not even the most pious of us is above temptation.

—**Loree Lough**, bestselling author of 100+ award-winning novels, including *Saving Alyssa* and *A Man of Honor*.

"I always expect the unexpected from Travis W. Inman, but this is something entirely different. I can only describe this writing as a spiritual "punch in the gut" in the best way possible for anyone who has fought and struggled with the issues so intuitively exposed and cleverly crafted in this book. This is not simply entertainment, but a ministry and wake-up call to anyone who is carelessly flirting with disaster. It has awakened me and changed me in ways I am still trying to figure out!"

—**Gil Maza,** Law Enforcement Chaplain

"*Shadows* is one of the most powerful books I have read; this is the first one in a while that I can't close and forget. Travis W. Inman has written a story that pictures so clearly what effect our choices, good and bad, have not only on us but on those around us."

—**Ann Ellison**

"Shadows is an important book—Travis W. Inman gives the reader the opportunity to foresee the impact of one man's choice. The characters are real and the story is fast-paced and captivating."

—**Sheryl Quesnel**

"Inman's tale is a gritty, realistic look at the importance of one's choices in life, about the consequences we bring on ourselves, and the hope we have when we lean on God for direction. A compelling, satisfying story that leaves the reader reconsidering his own decisions."

—**Robin Bayne**, Carol Award-winning author of
The Artist's Granddaughter. "

Travis Inman's latest Christian-themed novel presents the universal question: what harm comes from a brief affair? After reading *Shadows*, the answer is clear: all harm, no gain. I enjoyed the dual timeline format, the crisp writing, and the lessons taught, even if the characters may not have realized the same truths as the readers. I look forward to Travis' stories, and recommend *Shadows* to all readers who enjoy exploring "what if" situations."

—**Tom Jones III**

"*Shadows* is a fascinating tale that shows how one choice changes life – better or worse – for generations to come. It is a gripping story of sin, loss, redemption and hope. A must-read!"

—**Joshua Hardt**

"Our choices greatly effect who we are and what we do in life, and *Shadows* is a perfect example of that! At first I thought it was an adult oriented book, but as I continued reading, I realized that *Shadows* should be read by young adults and teens. Inman skillfully addresses common struggles and helps prepare young people to be ready to face those issues before they choose the wrong path."

—**Richard Cowell**

Shadows

—One Choice a Future Makes—

Travis W. Inman

Elk Lake Publishing

Shadows: One Choice a Future Makes
Copyright © 2015 by Travis W. Inman

Requests for information should be addressed to:
Elk Lake Publishing, Atlanta, GA 30024
ISBN-13 Number: 978-1-942513-62-9

Cover and graphics design: Anna M. O'Brien

Editor: Deb Haggerty

All references to New Life Ministries, *Women in the Battle*, and *Every Man's Battle* are used with permission.

ACKNOWLEDGMENTS

My Focus Group:
Dave, Alison, Shelley, Janis, Shara, and Sheryl.

Alex Wilson for his excellent advice on all things military.

THE BEGINNING

Gerald held a lit match to his pipe, stole a glance at Walter through a gray tendril of smoke, and then turned his attention to Dahlia, his eyes heavy with regret. The woman standing before them was dangerous. Her beauty made her desirable and her job made her deadly. Only the strongest could resist her. If a man carried a secret vulnerability, she would exploit it, and he would never realize what happened. Gerald caught Walter's eyes again and tried to smile, but his lips were plastic. "Do you understand what we are asking of you?"

Dahlia examined the two older men sitting in wing-backed chairs and leaned forward, her ample bodice threatening to release, causing Gerald to look at his shoes. Her throaty voice made them press further into their chairs. "Married men are easy; you barely have to offer them what they know they want and they will do anything you ask of them."

Gerald's scowl started from his throat. "Once he walks away, you are to stand down. Do you understand me? If he says no, then you stop."

Dahlia turned her eyes into Gerald's glare. "How aggressively shall I approach him?"

"For this to work, you have to be an assassin. Get close. Get personal. But when he declines, get out."

Dahlia's expression was thick with amusement. "And when he can't turn me down?'"

"If he fails? Then he's your mouse to play with."

"Agreed." She stepped back and allowed the men to breathe again. "My normal fee; my normal arrangements. I expect payment immediately."

Gerald lifted his phone and pressed a button. "So be it. That will be all."

"Gentlemen, as always, it's a pleasure doing business with you." She didn't have to look back to know they were watching her make her exit.

Walter swallowed and lifted his hand to signal the waiter. His eyes narrowed and his lips puckered. "She's vetted?"

"We've used her before. She's familiar with our confidentiality standard. She won't be a problem." He tugged at his pipe again. "She's very good."

The waiter approached carrying a small wooden cigar box on a silver tray and extended the tray to the older, pot-bellied man. "May I light your cigar, Mr. Bigger?"

"That won't be necessary." He reached into the box, selected the longest of the cigars, and gently squeezed with his fingers. He found the cutter on the tray and snipped the end of his cigar. He fumbled in his pocket for a book of matches and nodded at the waiter. "That will be all." He turned his gaze to Gerald and watched him over the edge of a lit match, which he held to his cigar. "Is this the same woman who took down the Speaker of the House?"

Gerald's forehead creased at the memory. "One and the same."

Walter puffed his cigar twice. "She's magnificent. Truly a rose with a thorn."

"Actually, she's a thorn with a bloom. A Venus flytrap," he said with regret. "Very few men can resist her." Gerald lifted the pipe to his lips. "The whole matter is quite distasteful."

Walter shrugged. "The cost of doing business. Besides, this was your idea. He's your man, not mine."

Gerald mused for a moment. "I think he's the one. Our future rests with him."

"*Our* future?"

"Your future is entangled with mine. As is everyone's." He intertwined his fingers for effect. "We're only as strong as our weakest link."

"And you think Justin Grey can prevail."

Gerald exhaled slowly. "I will speak to him at the conference and make a final determination. But, were I to place a bet, I'd wager the farm on him."

"Well, that's exactly what you're doing." Bigger blew smoke across the room. "It's your legacy. We like him. We like his family. We all agree."

Gerald nodded. "Then it's done."

CHAPTER ONE
Justin "Flip" Grey

By the time Norm took the stage at the 53rd Annual Hilton Head Bank and Market Conference, the crowd had already begun to enjoy the open bar at the back of the room. They always made an elegant assortment of fine liquors available on the opening night of the conference, as if a banking conference wouldn't be fun without it. But Norm was the man who made the conference fun. He deliberately told miserable jokes that were over the top—real groaners! "A robber walks up to the teller and hands her a note that says, 'hand over all your money, or you'll be geography.' The teller looks at him and says, 'you mean history,' to which the robber replies, 'don't change the subject.'"

This year, he wore an electric tie resembling a foot-long hot dog with radioactive mustard glowing bright yellow. Norm was the man everyone wanted to know, and almost everyone, including sour-faced bank presidents, found themselves laughing at his genuinely humorous antics.

He tapped on the microphone and said, "Ladies and Gentlemen, welcome to the 53rd Hilton Head conference. We appreciate all of you taking the time to join us for the most exciting bank conference available.

"I know you're looking for great entertainment. First of all, we have this awesome South Carolina beach!"

The audience cheered enthusiastically.

"I'll take any chance I am offered to spend a few days sitting in the sun and soaking in the awesome Atlantic sea water. And I must brag on our host, the Westin Resort. I challenge anyone to find better facilities in all of the United States."

He held up his smartphone and said, "Let me tell you about something I saw on the news as I was driving here this afternoon. The janitor at the First National Bank in Justice, Texas, was emptying the trashcans at the end of the day when would-be robbers burst through the door. The janitor was so frightened he ran out the door, jumped into the first car he saw, and drove to the police station, which was only a few blocks away. It turns out the janitor jumped into the crooks' getaway car! The cops found them walking on the sidewalk trying not to look suspicious … I suppose the black masks made it hard to blend in."

He paused a moment and allowed the high-spirited audience to realize he was changing directions.

"I am glad to see you here again this year. It's always fun to see the same faces, even if they belong to you. We always start our conferences with a fun night. Most of you either flew in or drove in today and Sunday is not really an official night of the conference. This is our meet and greet time when you get to sample some of the truly fantastic local barbecue, have a few drinks on us, and unwind after a long day of travel. Tomorrow morning will start our conference. We'll get started at nine o'clock in the morning. The way I look at it, we're bankers after all! Why shouldn't we observe banker's hours?

"On this year's agenda, we offer cutting-edge topics such as the evolution and characteristics of community banks, lessons learned, and successful strategies for the community bank of the future. Additional topics include Tax and Regulatory Reporting, Accounting Methods and Principles, and Implications of Tax Reform. Personally, I can't wait for Wednesday! Implications of Tax Reform really gets my engine revved up! Then we have the Capital Markets Tax Developments. Well, you will find out about all those awesome topics when you register in the morning. Personally, I don't care if you even bother to register as long as you pay. That's the bottom line to me!

"Again, Sunday is considered to be a fun day, so let's get back to not thinking about taxes or regulations. Every day of the conference, we will have a rising star in the banking industry introduce themselves to the group. They will give their short overview of how they're taking banking into the future. Honestly, this is one of the things that makes our conference the best. You get a chance to hear from ordinary men and women who are strategic thinkers.

"Well, tonight we've asked Justin Grey to start us out. I've known Justin for at least ten years. Talk about an ordinary man—Justin fits the bill. And I mean that as a compliment. He's an ordinary man, who is becoming an extraordinary banker. Justin is an investment advisor at Panhandle State Bank in Sandpoint, Idaho. I know Idaho is known for its potatoes, but it's also known for its gems. And Justin is one of those gems. He likes skiing, football, and coin collecting. He loves to hunt and fish, and he loves to barbecue whatever he brings home. And I do know he loves to laugh and enjoy life. I also know this, his nickname is Flip, but that's a story he should tell you over a beer as you bankers wouldn't appreciate a sordid story about one of your own. Please join me in welcoming Justin "Flip" Grey."

Norm looked to his left and extended a welcoming hand to Justin, who began making his way to the podium.

"I've got 'em warmed up for you, Flip, the rest is up to you."

He slapped Justin on the shoulder, handed him the microphone, and exited the stage leaving Justin awkwardly holding the mike. Justin wore a sports coat but no tie. He resembled the popular kid at school who had a fashionable haircut and rugged smile. He wasn't flashy, but he was competent. He was also nervous and the crowd knew it.

"Hello, my name is Justin Grey and I am, uh, from Idaho. Yes, the potato state," he said with a boyish grin. "It's a long-held tradition to have ordinary bankers make a short presentation about what we're doing locally and I know we're required to present a PowerPoint, uh, presentation." He pressed a button on the clicker in his hand and the screen behind him came to life. "This is my local bank in Sandpoint, Idaho, which is in the panhandle of the state." He pressed another button and continued.

"This is my home. We named it Pinehurst because it was a house that deserved a name." Several nods of approval moved through the audience as they saw the magnificent house the Greys called home. "I don't live in Sandpoint, but in Bonners Ferry, which is just north of Sandpoint near the Canadian border ... eh?" He laughed nervously. "I paused a moment before saying *eh* just to emphasize how closely connected we are with Canada, but more on that in a little while." He pressed the button and continued.

"Here you see me with my wonderful wife, Connie. We've been married now for almost thirteen years. She works as a teller at my bank, and it's *always* fun to be near your wife every day." The way he said *always* made the crowd chuckle. "These are my incredible kids, starting with my daughter, Ginger. We have no idea how she got red hair. As you can see, both my wife and I have dark hair." That comment prompted some cat calls from near the bar. He smiled and said, "I choose not to think about it!" which spurred additional laughter. "Ginger just turned twelve last week. And this is my son, Kevin, who is about to turn eleven. And there in the background you can see my other kid, our three-year-old beagle, Gracie. I'm not sure which one I'm proudest of.

"I, uh, don't want to, uh, steal Norm's thunder, but I did hear some breaking news myself on the flight over." He reached into his pocket, produced a sheet of paper, and looked sheepish. "I even took a moment to write down this breaking news so I could share it with you." He glanced at his notes. "I'm an investment advisor, and as I hinted earlier, I do have an interest in investing in Canada. But I have to tell you," he held up his paper for emphasis. "I have to warn you about this breaking news in Japan.

"As you're aware, the Tokyo Stock Exchange plummeted on Friday causing widespread panic in Japan. As a result, the Origami Bank has folded, the Sumo Bank has gone belly up, and the Bonsai Bank announced plans to cut some of its branches." He paused a moment while the crowd roared with laughter.

"The Karaoke Bank is up for sale and will likely go for a song while shares in the Kamikaze Bank were suspended after they nose-dived." Again he had to pause.

"This is all true. I promise. Meanwhile, the Samurai Bank is soldiering on following sharp cutbacks and the Ninja Bank is reported to have taken a hit, but they remain in the black." He stopped for a moment while the laughter continued.

"There's more if you can stand it." He glanced at Norm, who was holding his chest and gasping for breath. "You all right, Norm?" Norm waved him off and held a thumb up. "Okay, I'll try to make this quick." As he looked at his paper, he had to fight back his own laughter, which made the crowd love him even more.

"It seems ..." he broke up for a moment and then steeled himself. "It seems five hundred staff at the Karate Bank got the chop ..." He paused a moment and caught his breath. "And analysts report there is something fishy going on at the Sushi Bank where it is feared the staff may get a raw deal!" That did it. The whole house erupted into an uproar while half-drunk bankers slapped each other on the backs and gasped for breath.

Justin allowed them a minute to enjoy the levity and then continued. "In all sincerity, do you know the difference between an investment advisor and a large pizza? Yep, the large pizza will feed a family of four!" The crowd loved him even though he turned his presentation to the direction he was trying to take his bank to meet the needs of the future.

He spoke to them for twenty minutes more about the investment services he was providing such as the making of markets, trading of derivatives and equity securities. He spoke about FICC services, such as fixed income instruments, currencies, and commodities.

There were many things Justin didn't tell them, personal things that the bankers wouldn't care about. Such as the fact he had taught the married couples' Sunday school class for the past three years. Or that he had a mediocre relationship with God even though he appeared to be a stalwart spiritual leader.

For the most part, he was moderately disciplined and had never needed to be more so. He loved his wife and kids but had wandering eyes that saw all the women around him. He didn't want to have an affair or even have any interactions with other women, but he always wondered about those things in the back of his mind. He openly spoke against pornography and adultery, while secretly fighting his own personal demons of lust from within.

Truth be told, he'd never really developed a meaningful relationship with his wife, who desired more than anything to be his soul mate. Sometimes he was a little grumpy with her, but not always. And if he were honest, he would admit he was a little resentful his wife put on a few pounds after Kevin was born. Connie was still an attractive woman even though she carried twenty extra pounds. But Justin himself was an average man, neither handsome nor homely. His greatest asset was his smile. His genuine, rugged smile made people like him instantly.

Justin also didn't tell people that once, in high school, he was at a football party and was goaded into getting drunk by his teammates. The experience was horrible and he swore never to get drunk again. As he never developed a taste for alcohol, he very seldom drank.

When he finished his speech, the bar in the back of the room closed and the group made their way to the various lounges scattered throughout the Westin Resort. As he descended from the stage, Norm greeted him with a warm handshake. "That was awesome, Flip. Just awesome."

Justin smiled gratefully. "Thanks, Norm. I appreciated your offer to let me speak."

"It was our pleasure, Flip." Norm paused and looked at him funny. "You don't mind if I call you Flip, do you? You seemed irritated by it."

"Well, to be honest, Flip was a nickname I earned for being a bonehead. I don't use my nickname anymore."

Norm held up a hand. "No hard feelings? I thought you went by that name all the time."

"Oh, I used to. But in the last few years, most folks just call me Justin."

"Good enough for me, Justin," Norm nodded in approval. "Some of us are going down to the cigar lounge for some smokes and a glass of cognac. Won't you join us?"

"My pleasure." He'd been hoping for such an opportunity. He'd heard there was a cigar club that was an elite group—invitation only. He knew inclusion in such a group would open many new doors for him in his future, and he was eager for the opportunity.

"Say, do you golf, Justin?"

"Oh, I've been known to swing a club or two in my day."

"Excellent. We're getting a group together for tomorrow afternoon, say around three?"

"I'll be there." He knew the Westin offered unforgettable golf and he'd brought his clubs just on the off chance he would get an opportunity to hit a few balls.

After a short walk down the hall, Norm paused at an unmarked door and pulled out a small silver key. "Here we are. We have a quiet spot where we won't be bothered by unnecessary interruptions. Welcome to the *Lair*."

The room was as stuffy as one would expect a cigar and cognac socialization room to be. The wooden walls and the pockets of wing-backed chairs revealed this was a club that went back several generations. He was surprised to see it wasn't a true gentleman's club—he saw several women scattered throughout the room chatting with their male counterparts.

As they entered the room, a distinguished gentleman approached holding a smoldering pipe in one hand. He extended a friendly handshake to Justin with the other. He was a man with slightly graying temples and kind but perceptive eyes. Justin felt very little probably got past him. "Ah, the man of the hour has arrived!" the man said with enthusiasm.

Norm stepped forward and said, "Mr. Alexander, I would like to introduce you to Justin Grey. Justin Grey, meet Gerald Alexander."

"How do you do, Mr. Grey?"

"I am well, thank you." He paused a moment and said, "Thank you for inviting me to join you this evening."

"We're glad to have you. Glad to have you. Say that was a magnificent speech you gave this evening. Splendid, in fact. The Sushi Bank killed me." He didn't wait for Justin to reply, "Won't you walk with me? I want to introduce you to the rest of the Lair."

"I'll take my leave," Norm said. "Gerald was right, Justin. That was a magnificent speech. I have other fish to fry, so to speak, so I will say good night."

"Have a good evening, Norm," Gerald gestured goodbye to him and then turned to Justin. "We have quite a collection of bankers here in the room. They're looking forward to meeting you."

"*The Lair*?" He asked.

Gerald almost seemed dismissive. "Oh, that's what we like to call ourselves. We're mostly just a harmless group of men and women who think alike and want to see our clients prosper as much as possible—and ourselves, to boot," he added with a wink. He puffed on his pipe and Justin caught a whiff of … licorice?

Justin couldn't help but think of him as the Godfather. Gerald had an air about him that told anyone who paid attention he was a man of great standing amongst his peers. Gerald led him to a potbellied man with a long cigar who was talking to a group of fussy-looking gray-haired gentlemen. Justin found himself hoping the old men wouldn't die before he had a chance to meet them. In his mind, he compared Potbelly to Boss Hogg.

As he approached, Gerald cleared his throat, "Gentlemen, allow me to introduce Justin Grey to you." One by one, he announced their name and they formally shook his hand accompanied by a polite, "how do you do?" The first introduction was to Walter Bigger, then Sam Summer, Edward Robinson, and finally Luke Dressler. He endured several more comments about his clever speech and Walter, who sported the potbelly, grabbed him by the shoulders with both hands and leaned in towards him. One look into Walter's eyes and he gave up the notion about Boss Hogg. Justin tried not to cough when he accidentally inhaled some of the drifting cigar smoke.

"Son, that was a masterfully delivered speech," Bigger drawled with a distinct Southern accent. "We want you to know we've been keepin' our eyes on you for quite a while and we're impressed with what we've seen. We'd enjoy getting' to know you better if you're of mind to do so. If you promise not to embarrass us old men, we'd like to take you golfin' tomorrow afternoon. They have a dogleg on the ninth hole that's a killer, but a young man like you should be hittin' one on the green from the tee box if he wanted to. What do you say?"

"Well, sir, I'm humbled you would want to know me. And I'm honored to play with you." He looked around, "All of you. Thank you for taking an interest in me."

Walter looked up at Gerald. "You were right about this one. He's a very genuine soul. I like him already." He patted Justin on the shoulder and then ambled off to the bar to order a drink. The other old men shuffled along behind him.

If Justin was confused before, he was most certainly confused now. Gerald could see that look in his eyes and said, "Come on, I have a few more people to introduce to you and then we can take a few minutes and chat if you like."

Justin mustered a smile. "Sounds like a good thing to do."

"Shall we?" Together, they made the rounds of the sizeable room. Justin counted roughly thirty men and four women to whom he was introduced. He endured many of the same pleasantries as before. He certainly had the impression they were waiting for him specifically. Although each member of the group had a drink in their hands, none of them appeared to be inebriated in the least. Finally, he and Gerald could sit and talk.

"Well, what do you think of our little group?"

Justin glanced around the room again searching for the right answer. "To be honest, I'm a bit confused. They seem like an extraordinary group of men. And women, of course. Well, I should say, professionals. Yes, that's what …"

Gerald smiled warmly. "Relax. I know what you mean. Meeting this group can be a bit intimidating—and even being a part of it can be. That's why we introduce by name alone for the first time. If you knew who all the professionals were, you wouldn't have agreed to come. For example, take Walter there. He might have a pot belly and appear to be rather harmless, but he is our delegate to the Bilderberg Group. Sam Summer is our representative to the Freemasons. Edward Robinson is a member of the Knights Templar—the original group, mind you, not the modern offshoot of the Masons." He paused a moment, which allowed Justin a moment to think.

Finally, Justin asked, "But the Knights Templar were disbanded many years ago, weren't they?"

Gerald almost laughed. "Don't tell that to Edward. He'd have a heart attack. He will explain all of that to you someday … perhaps. He's funny about the society sometimes, so don't pry."

"I wouldn't dream of it." He shifted in his chair. "And what about you? Do you belong to something secret too?"

"I belong to Skull and Bones." Gerald removed his ring to show Justin. "And before you ask, yes, I went to school at Yale and I do know George Bush." Gerald studied him for a moment and said, "I can imagine you're wondering what all this is about, but you don't know how to ask the proper question."

"In fact, I am."

"And you might also be a little concerned you're now in danger of being killed if you know too much about this group."

"Well," Justin struggled with a response. "I certainly am now."

Gerald's smile was disarming. "No fear. We're not that kind of group. But before we get into details, would you care for a drink?"

Justin held up his hands apologetically. "I'm sorry. I don't drink."

"Never?" Gerald asked, his eyebrow rising.

"Well, seldom."

"Won't you join me for some Scotch? I have some Auchentoshan 1957, which is superb."

"Uh, okay," Justin conceded, "I don't want to be rude."

"Nonsense." He lifted his hand and then two fingers. Justin couldn't see who he was signaling. But in less than a minute, a formally clad waiter approached carrying a silver tray with two crystal tulip glasses, which he sat on their small, round, claw-legged table. Gerald lifted his glass and sniffed deeply. "I always detect red apples."

Justin followed suit and sampled the aroma. "Hmmm. I smell peaches."

His comment made Gerald smile. "This '57 scotch is getting harder to find, so enjoy. He raised his glass in a salute. "Here's to new friendships."

Justin responded in like manner. "New friendships, indeed." He sipped the whiskey and was taken aback by its flavor. "Amazing." He held his glass closer to examine the contents.

"It's one of a kind, that's for sure."

"It's almost sweet," Justin replied.

"But it gets drier, almost nutty, at the finish."

"It's very nice. Thank you for sharing with me."

Gerald stopped and examined him for several seconds without comment. Finally, he said, "Justin, I've been following your career for several years now. You have an instinct for this job, which makes you a very gifted analyst. Moreover, you demonstrate true compassion and deep regard for your clients. Sometimes you talk people out of investing by explaining they simply can't afford to make the investment right then. That demonstrates a high degree of integrity. Most bankers would grab the money regardless of the outcome."

Justin wanted to ask how Gerald acquired such knowledge but held his tongue. He was more anxious to know what was going on and what part he was to play.

"You're a man of principle as well. You've been faithful to your wife and you love your children. You always take off your hat for the national anthem and place your hand over your heart when the colors are displayed. You are the kind of man we're looking for. With men like you, we can build a future."

Justin scratched his chin. "But I have nothing to offer you. Obviously, the men and women in this room have deep connections and influence. I'm just an ordinary man from North Idaho."

"That's where you're wrong. We're always looking for new members. We older men will eventually die off. We're not the kind of men who sit behind smoke-filled doors in some out-of-the-way country plotting to take over the world. Instead, we sit behind smoke-filled doors here and contemplate how to save our country. We're a group of professionals who believe integrity and honor should be our driving force. We're a group who believe a moral compass can only point in one direction. We're not trying to get you into a bloody cult that will demand your allegiance or your death. In fact, most of us are men of faith, who want to surround ourselves with more men and women who think like we do. The only exception is Giselle, who is French, and who is a priestess with Ordo Templis Orientis." He glanced at the slender, almost mousey woman chatting with another woman in the corner. "She follows a religion called Thelema. But she is most assuredly an American at heart. We're all the "local kid who made good" and we want to see others do so as well." Gerald sipped his whiskey. "I am a local businessman as you are. I'm from Spokane, Washington, just over an hour's drive from Sandpoint. I attend the First Baptist Church. I'm also the president of Washington Bank and Investment Group. If you're interested, I would like to offer you my services."

"Well, I'm always looking for a new business contact—"

"I don't think you understand what I'm offering you," Gerald interrupted with a lifted hand. "I'm talking about taking you on as my partner in the Lair. Sort of a mentorship if you will. I can help you get established with the group. Of course, it's completely up to you."

Justin was stunned and didn't know how to respond. "I ... uh... To be honest, I don't know how to react. I just can't imagine why you would be interested in me of all people. Lots of ethical, Christian businessmen out there would jump at the chance to be a part of something like ... this."

"Your hesitancy confirms for me you're the right choice. We don't want power-hungry people or those looking for someone to make them rich. That's not who we are. I'm a very wealthy man. I use my wealth to invest in the Kingdom. I support ten full-time missionary families in different parts of the world. My wealth is meaningless to me because I have my priorities on less temporal things."

Justin listened carefully. Gerald's words made him consider where his life was going and what he wanted to accomplish. He sipped his Scotch and thought about their conversation. How would he react if he were as wealthy as Gerald? "Well," he finally replied after several minutes of silent contemplation. "I am interested. What's expected of me?"

"That's an excellent question, Justin. However, I can't officially sign you up just yet. There are a couple of housekeeping items we need to discuss. Items of a private sort, if you will."

Justin shifted in his chair. "That sounds ominous."

Gerald leaned toward him. "Oh, it is. I'm going to get downright personal once you tell me I can."

Perplexed by the statement, Justin finally blurted out, "What do you mean?"

"I have a few concerns about your personal life. You have some vulnerable areas. If you have the courage, we'll discuss them and tighten the bolts, so to speak. You know, knock some of the rust off."

"Well, that doesn't really answer my question."

Gerald sighed. "Unfortunately, unless you give me permission to speak about your life, I can go no further. The choice is yours."

Justin's mind spun as he contemplated what in his life made him vulnerable. He had not performed any illegal investments, nor executed any tricky tax maneuvers. For the life of him, he couldn't imagine what Gerald knew about him that could be so damning. And there was also the implication he would need courage to face his evils. Finally, he landed on a question. "What happens if I tell you to proceed, but I don't want to discuss whatever you have on your mind?"

Gerald nodded in approval. "See, you know how to ask questions that cut right to the core of the issue. I'll discuss one major issue with you at a time. And don't worry, there aren't that many. If you become overwhelmed, you can back out. But I think I know you well enough to realize you aren't that weak. You're a man of substance." Gerald examined him carefully. "Why did you just smile? What was funny?"

Justin shook his head and looked down at the floor. "How can I not allow you to reveal my sins to me after you spent all that time building me up?"

Gerald's eyes smiled. "You're perceptive. I'm very careful with my words. I've found people are willing to face their demons if they know they're not alone and they're strong enough to endure. If you just split a man open, he will bleed until he dies. If you cut with precision, the wound will bleed, but the bleeding will be controlled. You're not my first mentorship. That trophy belongs to Norm. He was a mess when we first brought him on." He chuckled under his breath. "He still has his moments."

Justin mentally distanced himself and searched his heart. He knew he wanted this opportunity, but did he have the heart to hear the truth? And what would happen to him if he heard the truth but then suppressed the knowledge? Would that make him a worse man than he was before he was confronted? He reached into the depths of his spirit and said, "Okay. I'm in."

"Let's have another scotch." Gerald motioned to the bar again. "I promise to make this as easy as possible." Once they'd had their glasses refreshed, he said, "From my research, you were attacked at your home just over a year ago."

Justin was startled. "Attacked?"

Gerald's eyes told him to be still and listen. "Yes, attacked—by the very depths of evil and depravity. And it was a surgical strike, I might add. Last June, you were researching a new resort proposal in Nelson, British Columbia, late on a Friday night—just twelve minutes past midnight, to be precise. In your Internet research, you triggered a pop-up ad offering a free visit to a porn site. To your credit, you didn't bite. However, the pop-up ad stayed on your screen for more than a minute, which told them you were considering the offer. One month later, the same pop-up ad hit your computer, only this time you followed the link."

Justin closed his eyes and exhaled deeply. Gerald paused to let him collect his thoughts.

"That's funny. I thought this was going to be about an illegal tax loophole or something. I had no idea you were going to be this personal."

Gerald nodded. "It's *the little foxes that spoil the vine*. You didn't visit the site very often, but you visited. And as Matthew 5:28 tells us, if you look upon a woman with lust, then you have already committed adultery in your heart. The problem became an issue when your wife noticed you had not come to bed by two o'clock in the morning. Even though she didn't know you were doing something wrong, she caught you. And you lied to her. That lie set you on a dark path. You started frequenting the site shortly after. Besides being a sin against God, your actions were a sin against her and your family. You became dissatisfied with your wife—always comparing her to the airbrushed super models on your website. She can't measure up to them. And moreover, she suspects something is wrong. You've progressed to the point where you would rather spend time with your fantasy women than make love to your wife."

Justin didn't realize Gerald had stopped talking. His mind was reeling and he felt as though he was going to be sick. Gerald had pressed on a wound that had been festering in his heart for several months. He was already under conviction for his behavior and he knew he was wrong. How could he go from such a high following his speech to such a low only an hour later?

Gerald seemed to know his thoughts and said, "Well, there it is. The ugly part is over. Once your sin is brought to light, you can take action. You now have a decision. Either you accept the evil of your sin and repent, or you suppress your sin and sink further into depravity. I'll leave you with one thought: There is nothing you can do God won't forgive. No matter how far away from Him you walk, He's only one step away."

He held up his hand again and the waiter brought him a book on the silver platter. He held the book for a moment and then spoke quietly. "If it makes you feel any better, I tend to struggle with the same problem.

This book helped me greatly." He held it up for Justin to see: *Every Man's Battle* by Steve Arterburn and Fred Stoeker. "I would also recommend *Every Man's Battle Workshop*, which just happens to be going on this week in Atlanta. I placed some information about the workshop in the book." He extended the book to Justin, who stared weakly at it. "I want you to have this. You're not alone. You can overcome this. You can get your life back on track. I'll help you."

He placed his empty glass on the table. "I'll retire for the evening now." He examined his pipe. "Besides, my pipe has already gone to sleep; I should head that way myself. Justin?" He waited until Justin was looking at him. "Thank you for the privilege of trusting me. I believe in you and I know you have it in you to do the right thing. I'll take my leave now and we can speak in the morning. If you wish, come back here and join me for breakfast at seven sharp." He placed a grandfatherly hand on Justin's shoulder and almost appeared to be praying for him. "Good night."

Gerald turned to walk away and then hesitated and said, "One last word. Be very careful. I've opened a wound and you're now vulnerable. Keep that in mind and take it easy for the rest of the night."

CHAPTER TWO
Justin "Flip" Grey

Connie listened to him with enthusiasm while Justin described how successful his speech had been. "I don't want to brag, but I knocked them out. And those jokes about the Japanese banks went over better than I imagined. Having Norm handy with his horrible jokes to set the stage helped." As they talked, he strolled along the boardwalk that led from the resort to the beach. The tide had gone out, leaving more of the beach to walk. He turned toward an ungroomed area of the sand and slowly made his way along the water's edge. The smell of the salty water and the warm, moist breeze spoke to him, calling him to be at peace with himself again—to be at peace with God again.

Connie asked him, "So, tell me about the group you visited this evening."

"Well, I don't really know much about them other than they're some kind of secret society that wants to make America a better place. They appear to be a loose coalition of mostly Christian businessmen. They have offered me membership in their club. It's called the Lair."

"*The Lair*? That sounds kind of scary."

"I know, right?"

"Are you going to join them?"

"Well, they're recruiting me. I guess they haven't actually offered me membership yet. At least I don't think so. It's hard to tell."

"What does that mean?"

"Hmmm. I'm not sure how to explain it. They want me to go through a sort of vetting process. It's hard to explain."

"This doesn't sound very good to me." Connie's voice demonstrated her concern.

"You had to be there to understand it."

"So, what are you going to do?"

"To be honest, I'm not sure. I really want to join them. I think it would be a great thing for me … and for us. It's just a little complicated."

"Can you explain to me why you're concerned? Are they asking you to do something inappropriate?"

"No. Nothing like that. They want to make sure I'm their kind, that's all."

"Their kind? What does that mean?"

"I can't really describe it." The wound in his heart was still raw. He was aching deep inside with the grief over what he'd done. He wanted to explain to Connie what was actually happening, but at the same time, he had been pushing her away for so many months that simply reversing course seemed impossible. Besides, the embarrassment of his secret … of his sin, was hard to swallow. He wasn't sure if he had the wherewithal to open up more tonight. Maybe tomorrow.

"Honey, please tell me what's going on. I'm worried you're going to get sucked up into something that's not right."

"No, it's nothing like that. I think these are good people."

"Well, they certainly don't sound too good right now."

Justin closed his eyes and shook his head in frustration at being unable to explain. "Nothing bad is happening," he said with more edge to his voice than he intended. "They just want to be sure I'm a good fit for them."

"Well, of course, you're a good fit. It's not like you've done anything wrong."

"Yeah," he replied half-heartedly.

"Justin? You haven't done anything wrong, have you?" Now *her* voice had an edge.

"No! Of course not." Did he just lie to her? He knew she meant legally—she couldn't possibly suspect a spiritual or integrity issue to be at play. Still, his answer felt like a lie. The truth was, he *had* done something wrong. He rolled his head back on his shoulders. He didn't need this kind of stress tonight. Not from Connie. Not tonight.

"Then why am I worried?"

Annoyance in his voice, he replied, "I don't know why you're worried, Connie."

She was silent and offered no further conversation. Now, what? Why was she giving him the silent treatment? Of all the rotten luck! He didn't need this. After an irritating minute of silence, he asked sharply, "What is it, Connie?"

"Nothing."

"No, it's not nothing. Tell me what's wrong." He was trying hard not to yell at her.

"It's just … well, what are you doing up there?"

"What do you mean, what am I doing? I'm talking to you on the phone."

"Where are you?"

"I'm walking on the beach."

She timidly asked, "Are you by yourself?"

"What?" He exploded. "What's that supposed to mean? Of course, I'm by myself! Who would I be with?"

"I didn't mean that, Justin. Forget I said it." He was seething. "How dare you accuse me of being unfaithful? Have I ever done anything to justify that?"

"No, honey. I'm sorry, okay? I'm just feeling really uneasy about all this."

"I can't believe you asked if I was with someone. Why would you do that?"

"I don't mean it," she backpedaled. "You've just been very secretive lately, that's all. I don't really feel like you want to be around me anymore." She was starting to cry, which really hacked him off.

"Secretive? So you immediately conclude I'm cheating on you? Nice, Connie. Nice."

"I'm sorry, Justin. Okay? I'm sorry."

"You know what, Connie? I really didn't need this right now. I've got a lot on my mind. I can tell you having an affair is the last thing I want."

She didn't stop crying although he could hear her gulping as if she were trying. Justin listened to her for several awkward seconds. The longer she cried, the angrier he became. He finally ended the conversation abruptly, "I'll talk to you later. I've got to get to bed."

That didn't go well at all. He closed his eyes and lifted his face to the moonlight above. *How did I get out of control so quickly?* In his heart, he knew the argument was his fault. He had been secretive at home. He'd been secretive about viewing pornography, but how could he simply come out and say that? He wasn't certain if he should be angry at Gerald for stirring all of this up or if he should be angry at himself for creating the problem in the first place. *Aargh!* He didn't need this kind of pressure in his life.

He picked up a piece of driftwood and chunked it back into the sea. His eyes began to search the dimly lit beach for more things to throw when he noticed movement along the beach. He stopped and stared for a moment and then realized a person was walking there. In fact, he could tell it was a woman by her silhouette. He straightened up and watched her walking toward him.

She was close enough to him to speak. "Hello."

"Hello," he replied.

"You don't mind me being here, do you?"

"Uh, no, of course not. Why would I care?"

"Oh, I couldn't help but hear you talking on the phone and you sounded upset. I thought maybe you wanted to be alone?" She sounded nice. Her voice was pleasant and she had an easy way about her.

"I'm sorry I disturbed you."

She stepped closer to him. He could see her better and could make out she had long black hair that extended almost to her elbows. At first he thought she was slender, but now he could see she was stacked— extremely well-proportioned. Her long hair caught the breeze and lifted slightly around her. She reached up with her hands and attempted to smooth the wandering strands. "I'm sorry I accidentally overheard. I hope everything's okay." Her voice was even softer than before and very inviting.

He smiled shyly. "Nothing to worry about. Just a tiff with my wife." He turned to walk the other way. "I won't disturb you anymore."

"Wait a minute. Don't I know you?" she asked and stepped closer to see his face.

She was close enough for him to smell her perfume. Her scent was musky and perfectly complimented the beach. He couldn't help but breathe in again. *Nice.* "No, I don't think we've met. I'm pretty sure I'd remember." *Darn, I shouldn't have said that. It sounded flirty.*

Her smile was accented by the moonlight. "I do know you. You were the guest speaker tonight at the conference. Flip, right?"

"Uh, yes, that was me." *Now, what?* He felt awkward. And he needed to call and apologize to Connie.

She was now close enough to softly place a hand on his shoulder. "That was totally awesome! I haven't laughed so much in a long time. I felt really good listening to you."

Apparently he wasn't immune to shallow flattery. "Well, I ..." When she lifted her hand from his shoulder, he wished she hadn't.

"And your investment ideas. I have to say they border on genius. Your whole approach is inspiring."

"I'm just an ordinary guy trying to make a living." His head was starting to swim and he needed to place distance between them. "Have a good night."

"How lucky am I?" she continued. "I was hoping to run into you and tell you just how much I enjoyed seeing you today."

"Thank you. That's very flattering." He needed to leave, but for some reason he continued to look at her instead. She was so inviting. She looked wonderful. She was so ... tempting.

"My name is Dahlia."

"Justin," he replied weakly.

Her laugh was more of a throaty groan. "I know who you are." For the first time he saw she was carrying a bottle. She lifted it to her lips and drank. "Would you like some?"

He lifted his hand. "I can't. Really." *Come on you idiot*, he said to himself. *You need to get out of here. This woman is poison.*

"Are you kidding me? It's only wine. There's way too much for me to drink by myself. I was hoping to run into someone who might want to share. You aren't afraid, are you?"

"Afraid?"

"You aren't afraid of little ol' me, are you?" She wiggled her shoulders. She continued to lean close to him and brushed up against him slightly.

A breeze gusted past them, blowing her hair across her face and lifting her skirt. A thrill ran down his spine and caused him to shudder. He was being propositioned by a woman who could pass for a Victoria's Secret model. He glanced around. There was no one anywhere near him. They were alone. On the beach. Just the two of them. And a bottle of wine to boot. It would never be any easier. And he wanted it. He wanted her.

She moved closer—she rubbed against his chest. She had long legs, was almost as tall as he, and could almost look him in the eye. Her free hand ran down the length of her hair and then began to trace the lines of her body. Her perfume was drawing him closer. She seemed to want some attention from him. She lifted her bottle and took a long pull then handed him the bottle while her hand continued to tease along her curves.

"I'm thinking about a swim. Care to join me? She grabbed a handful of her shirt and slowly peeled it over her shoulders, revealing her black lace bra. "Take a drink. It's really good." She pressed the bottle closer to his lips and tried to pour the wine into his open mouth.

Suddenly his pocket began to vibrate as his cell phone came to life. He reached for the phone and saw "Connie" flash on the screen. "My wife …" he mumbled.

"You mean that woman who doesn't respect you? Get rid of her. I'll be undressing for our swim," she teased and reached to the front of her bra to unlatch the hooks. She had enough volume contained within the absence of the lace didn't expose any more of her than he could already see, which made him long to see more of her. She reached for his belt and began to tug.

Again the phone vibrated in his hand and he looked a second time at the screen. "Connie." Her call was about to go to voicemail.

CHAPTER THREE
Justin

He glanced from his phone to Dahlia's nearly naked body when she wiggled out of her skirt and dropped it on the sand near her shirt. His head was spinning and he felt as if this was happening to someone else.

The phone buzzed a third time. "Connie." She was probably calling to apologize. She probably felt horrible for accusing him falsely ... of cheating on her. She was making the first attempt to make things right between them before he went to bed for the night.

Dahlia artistically removed the last of her clothing and let the panty dangle from her fingers for a moment before letting it fall. Justin's eyes feasted upon her beauty for a second longer and then the phone rang for the fourth time. This was his last chance. If he delayed any longer, the call would go to voicemail. And he would be completely defenseless. He would submit.

He felt almost physical pain as he lifted the phone to his ear and stammered through dry lips, "Hello?"

"Hey, it's me," she paused a moment. "I was just calling to say I'm sorry. I know you would never cheat on me. I know you love me. Will you forgive me for being so childish?"

Connie's voice broke the spell Dahlia was casting over him, restoring him like a fresh breeze in the suddenly still, humid air. Consciousness was coming back to him; he ripped his eyes off Dahlia's goddess-like figure. He needed to get back to the safety of the lighted beach. He turned and started walking, slowly and then faster.

"Hello?" Connie wasn't sure he was on the line.

"Hey, it's me. Thanks for calling. I'm so sorry I got mad at you. I just had a very heavy weight on my mind and I was wrong." He had waited too long and now he would have to talk to her tomorrow. She would need to get to bed soon.

"What's going on?"

"Oh, it's too late to get into that now. You have to get up and go to work in the morning."

"Don't forget, I'm on Pacific Time. It's three hours earlier here."

He smiled. They had plenty of time. "Well, then, let's talk."

"Are you okay? You sound out of breath."

"I'm just walking on the beach trying to get back into the hotel."

"Are you enjoying the ocean?"

"Not so much. I'm ready to relax in my room."

"So, what's going on? You sound different."

"I think I am." As he walked, he came clean to her about Gerald and how he'd been confronted about his porn usage. She listened quietly until he was finished.

"I was wondering what was going on. You acted like you had a secret."

"I know, and I'm sorry. You can't imagine how stupid I feel and how embarrassed I am. But I promise you, it's over. I will not put myself through that again. Or you, either." The cloud of confusion and guilt was lifting from his mind. He was thinking clearly again.

"So, how's the beach? I've heard Hilton Head is awesome." Connie had wanted to join him on this trip, but with the kids and school, she couldn't.

"Well, the sharks are out tonight. There's more I need to tell you and it's as difficult as the first topic. You have no idea how glad I was you called when you did." He recounted a more PG version of his encounter with Dahlia. He finished with, "Connie, you have to understand how much I love you. I would never cheat on you, and I will make sure never to be in that situation again." She was silent and he couldn't tell what she was thinking or feeling. "Honey?" He could hear the tears in her voice.

"I'm here."

"Are you okay?"

"I think so." Her voice sounded sad and hollow.

"You understand I didn't do anything wrong, right?"

"But you did. Don't you see? You did. When you allowed her to get close to you. That could have been a disaster. That could have ended our lives as we know them. That could have destroyed everything we have and all that we are." She breathed deeply. "I know you didn't do anything wrong, but you almost did. I still feel betrayed."

He nodded. "You're right. Maybe I should come home."

Her answer surprised him. "Maybe you should."

His eyes caught on the book Gerald had given him earlier, *Every Man's Battle*. He flipped through the pages and found the brochure on the *Every Man's Battle Workshop*. His heart spoke to him; he suddenly knew what they needed to do. He read the brochure to her and said, "I think this is where I need to be rather than the bank conference. I need to be in Atlanta at *Every Man's Battle Workshop.* Google it and you'll see why."

"Okay, give me a minute … I'm looking at the workshop now. They also have something called *Women in the Battle Workshop*. Here's what they say about it on their website. '*The Women in the Battle Workshop* is designed to help women who have been hurt in relationships with men who are or have been involved in pornography, sexual addiction, or adultery. During this weekend of biblically-based teaching and small group process sessions, you will receive tools that can help you heal and rebuild your future.'"

"That sounds like you. It sounds like us. I think you should come."

"Justin, I can't just drop everything and come to Atlanta."

"Well, why not? Your sister can keep the kids or your mother can. You would have to drive through Coeur d'Alene to get to the airport anyway."

"Oh, I don't know. It's a lot of money to fly that far on short notice."

"We have the money."

"No, we don't."

He nodded aggressively. "Yes, we do. Just take it out of our hot tub fund."

"We can't do that! You really want a hot tub."

"What I want is for you to come here and for us to get things straightened out. Now get on a plane and come. I need you here."

At seven o'clock sharp the next morning, Justin walked down the hall and stood in front of the unmarked door. Before he could knock, the waiter opened the door from within and gestured him inside. Even though he knew the way, the waiter escorted him to Gerald's table. Gerald stood as they approached. "Ah, Mr. Grey. Won't you join me?"

"The first thing I want to say, sir, is thank you," he began while settling into his chair. "You exposed a dark spot in my soul that needed to be submitted to the light. I think shame was what kept me from doing the same thing myself."

Gerald agreed. "Shame can trap you into believing you can't escape. It's one of the most powerful emotions we possess."

"The second thing I want to say is I won't be able to keep our golf date."

His eyebrows lifted. "Oh?"

Justin nodded. "Yes, sir. I'm checking out of the conference and I will be attending *Every Man's Battle Workshop* in Atlanta."

Gerald was pleased. "I think that's fabulous. How very convenient both events were happening at the same time. Besides, you wouldn't get much out of this conference except a few legal updates and some stale jokes from Norm."

"Will you extend my regrets to the group?"

Gerald's eyes sparkled. He reached into his coat pocket and removed an envelope. "You will find I have already booked you into the workshop and you will find these accommodations will suit you and your wife. I've arranged for her to attend the accompaniment seminar, *The Women in the Battle Workshop.*"

"My wife? But, how could you know ..."

"All the arrangements have been made. Your wife will arrive this afternoon in Atlanta. She can attend her workshop and you can attend yours. And your lives will never be the same again." Gerald almost seemed to fight back tears.

Justin opened the envelope and thumbed through the papers. Everything was dated more than six months back. "But, how ... why ... what?"

"We believe in you, Justin. My wife and I did the same thing several years ago. That's when Walter Bigger, you remember him—the man with the big belly? He sponsored me to attend as well. Trust me, this is the right path for you." He lifted his hand for the waiter. "Mr. Grey and I will be having the eggs Benedict with smoked salmon." He glanced at Justin for approval. "They also have Canadian bacon if you'd rather?"

"No, so happens I like smoked salmon."

"Then it's settled." In a flash, their small table was set with coffee and juice. Justin casually glanced around the room and saw many of the members from the night before were filtering in for breakfast. Several stopped by their table and greeted him warmly. He felt like he belonged. He had come home.

CHAPTER FOUR
Flip

Again the phone vibrated in his hand. He looked at the screen. "Connie." The call was about to go to voicemail.

He glanced from his phone to Dahlia's nearly naked body when she wiggled out of her skirt and dropped it on the sand near her shirt. His head was spinning and he almost felt drunk as if this was happening to someone else.

The phone buzzed a third time. "Connie." She was probably calling to apologize. She probably felt horrible for accusing him falsely—of cheating on her. She was making the first attempt to make it right between them before he went to bed for the night.

Dahlia artistically removed the last of her clothing and let the panty dangle from her fingers for a moment before letting it fall. Justin's eyes feasted upon her beauty for a second longer and then the phone buzzed for the fourth time. This was his last chance. If he delayed any longer, the call would go to voicemail. And he would be completely defenseless. He would submit. He looked up from the phone and at Dahlia, who was beckoning to him with a finger. She was inviting him to come to her—to be her lover.

The phone stopped vibrating and the screen flashed, "1 Missed Call." He stuffed the phone in his pocket and lifted the wine to his lips. He had always wondered what sleeping with another woman would be like. This kind of opportunity didn't come along very often. She was something out of his website. He was living in a *Girls Gone Wild* video. A gorgeous, hot, available woman wanted him. She was so alluring and so tempting.

Besides, as Gerald mentioned earlier, if you look upon a woman and lust after her, you have already committed adultery in your heart. If he'd already committed the sin, why shouldn't he follow through? After all, a sin is a sin, right? And he could always repent when they were finished—after he had experienced all that she had to offer.

"Come on, Flip," she called to him. "I'm getting lonely out here."

He lifted the bottle to his lips again and drank deeply, allowing the wine to wash over him, preparing him for the pleasures ahead.

Dahlia paused at the water's edge and lifted her arms above her head, revealing how desirable she was. "Come on, lover. I'm waiting."

He almost ripped his shirt off as he raced to undress. She giggled and danced in front of him as he pulled off his pants. He confidently approached her and she fell into his arms.

He had a long, wonderful night. After frolicking on the beach, they stumbled into her room through the sliding glass door. She was really talented; she introduced things to him he had never known. He couldn't remember a more enjoyable evening in all of his life. This was what making love was meant to be. Love was supposed to be passionate and exciting and life-changing. Certainly not what he had at home. He only made love to his wife on weekends. Even then, he finished in a few minutes and then he would roll over and go to sleep. His wife didn't dance for him or tease him or make him desire her.

Dahlia poured wine into him and delighted him until they both passed out in the early morning hours. When he awoke, his head was pounding and his tongue felt like a furry stick in his mouth. Dahlia was draped near the foot of the bed. The sight of her body stirred him and he managed to sit up. She woke up, rolled over, and smiled, "Hey there, Lover."

"Morning," he muttered. He was feeling sick. How much had he drunk?

She wiggled closer to him and said, "Are you alright? You look a little green."

"I think I feel that way too," he managed to mumble despite his dry mouth.

She sat up and pulled her tangled hair behind her ears. She made no move to cover herself. "Go to the bathroom and get rid of the alcohol. You'll feel better. And then come take your medicine. Go on, now," she prompted when he didn't move. "Fine," she crawled over him and stood. "Come on. Let's get you back on your feet. You're no good to me in this state." She led him by the hand to the bathroom.

Once he was moving, nausea kicked in and he retched until all he had left were dry heaves.

"There, you probably feel better already." She turned on the shower and pushed him into it. "You'll be as good as new in no time." She watched him through the glass door and said, "My, you do look nice. Not a bad catch, if I say so myself. I think we make a great match. I'll be right back, lover. I'm going to make us a mimosa."

Coming back, she carried the drink with her and stepped into the shower too. "Here, drink this. A little hair of the dog that bit you will help."

He surrendered and lifted the glass to his dry lips. The drink was light and refreshing and soon he was feeling better. "Oh, my …" He was leaning against the shower wall. "What time is it?"

"I think it's about ten. Why?"

"We've got a conference. And we're late."

She laughed. "Don't be silly. This is what people come to conferences for. This is why they don't have important sessions early. We can still make the afternoon session if I can't tempt you into a day at the beach. We'll do whatever you want. I'm all yours and you're mine for a whole week. It's like a honeymoon, only we don't have to live together once the fun ends." She shut off the shower and threw a towel at him. "Now for some room service." He followed her from the shower and watched her slip into a robe. "This is what I intend on wearing today. How about you?"

"I need some coffee," he mumbled.

"Go sit on our patio. I'll bring you some." She gently pushed him and started him walking.

The sunlight and the rest of his mimosa stirred some life back into him. Slowly, he remembered. What was he doing? What had he done? He was almost in shock trying to remember all that happened the night before. How did it happen? And how could it be wrong when it felt so right? Shouldn't he feel guiltier than he did?

Before long, Dahlia came out with a cup of coffee and a new mimosa for him. "Thank you," he replied.

Dahlia examined him with laughing eyes. "This is your first time, isn't it?"

"First time?" He shook his head. "No, I'm married."

"Silly. I know you're married, that's why I liked you. I wanted a man who was tired of what he had at home. It makes him hungry for more. It makes him a great lover."

He didn't know what to say. *She targeted me?*

"For your first time, you did pretty well. A lot of first-timers leave during the night. Their guilty conscience gets to them. But it gets easier each time. Wait until you see what I have in mind for tonight. Or this afternoon, if we can't wait that long."

"I don't think I should …" he couldn't finish. What had he done? Conn … his wife …, was going to kill him.

Dahlia watched him struggle for a moment and then said, "Relax. You can go home to Mama and return to your comfortable life. I don't want you for anything but fun this week. I'll go home to my boring husband and you can go back to your boring job. Trust me, this is only for fun. I won't put a dead rabbit in your soup pot. Once we check out of here, we're done. Maybe we'll do it again at the next conference. Maybe we'll do someone else. We'll just have to see."

Flip felt his mind starting to spin. Everything in him said what he was doing was wrong, but Dahlia was making it seem so … enjoyable. There was no commitment. There was no consequence, His wife would never know. He could go home and step back right where he left off. Right? Was that possible?

Dahlia got up and went inside for a moment while he struggled with his situation. She came back with his cell phone. "Here, you better call your wife or she'll start to worry. Tell her how boring the conference is and how you can't wait to get back home. Tell her what she wants to hear."

He looked at the phone and saw he only had one missed call—the one from last night. Dahlia peeked over his shoulder. "See? Everything is all right. She didn't even bother to leave a message. I doubt she's even thinking about you."

"Why do you say that?"

"Because. She was ugly to you last night on the phone. If she really respected you, she wouldn't accuse you of doing things behind her back."

"How do you know about that?"

She playfully rolled her eyes at him. "Hello? I told you I was listening to you last night."

"You were?"

"Yep. I was following you until you got off the phone. I was waiting for you to get done with that meeting you had after your speech."

Oh, the meeting with the Lair! He was supposed to have had breakfast this morning with Gerald. Oh, well, surely he'd understand. It's not every night a man gets stalked by a sex nymph. "But why me?"

"Because. You looked good to me. I wanted you." She draped herself over his shoulder from behind. "I still want you." She tapped on the phone. "Now call your wife. I don't want you distracted."

He could feel her curves pressing against his neck and they felt good. He had never felt this alive. Ever. He lifted the phone to his ear and listened as it rang. "Hey, honey. How are you? Yes, I'm taking a break from what I'm doing." He glanced at Dahlia, who silently laughed at his remark and winked at him. "Yeah, I'm sorry, too. I was just tired. Let's not worry about it at all. We can just say it was a mistake and forget about it. I'm going to grab some lunch here pretty soon and I might even make it to the beach later today. I promise not to have fun without you." While he was talking, Dahlia straddled his lap and opened her robe enough for him to see. She started nibbling on his ear. "I miss you, too. Yes, I'll try to call later, but we do have some late meetings. I love you too, bye."

"See?" she said. "Nothing to it. This is only a game. We'll have fun and then we go home. It's that simple. No strings attached." A knock at the door got her back on her feet. "Room service is here. How does a pizza sound?"

Flip watched her cover herself with the robe again. "It actually sounds pretty good." Once he ate, he felt better and was up for more entertainment. Later, they put on their robes and walked down the beach to an isolated area where they swam. Several times, people walked past them, but they were in the water.

They made their way back to Dahlia's room, where she mixed some martinis and they took a nap. Flip had no idea having so much fun was so exhausting. When he remembered the golf date with the men from the Lair, he only had to glance at Dahlia and he was satisfied she was more fun than the old men. Besides, what did those tired old men have to offer?

The rest of his week continued in much the same fashion. He attended a few of the conference sessions, the ones about legal updates and new tax laws. For the most part, he and Dahlia spent their time immersed in the pleasures they could enjoy while they were together.

He never saw any of the Lair members the rest of the time he was there. Once, he ran into Norm in the hall, but Norm offered him little more than a pleasant, but abrupt, greeting and moved past him quickly. *Well, if that's the way the members of the Lair behave, then I'm better off without them. I've better things to do than to be playing up to them.* As far as Flip was concerned, they had shown their true colors and he was glad to be done with them.

On the last day of the conference, Flip and Dahlia parted just as planned. Flip had an early flight, so after their final liaison that evening, he went to his room and slept in his own bed. But he couldn't sleep. Not really. His mind started working once he relaxed. When he was with Dahlia, they were all action, no time for thinking. She was wonderful. And now that she didn't distract him, his mind engaged.

He lay looking up at the ceiling and wondered how hard it would be to return to his home … and his wife. He'd had a fantastic week playing with Dahlia and experiencing all the new things he'd finally gotten to enjoy. For the first time in his life, he felt he understood what love really was. And he realized he'd never really, truly loved Conn … his wife. They simply didn't make each other happy. Maybe they did at first, but no longer. And they deserved to be happy, right? He certainly knew now what being happy felt like. The week he'd spent with Dahlia was the most incredible week of his life. Why couldn't he find that kind of happiness again?

He knew one thing; he would never find that at home. He and Conn … his wife would never be able to be that happy. She wasn't that kind of woman. She didn't know how to make him happy the way his "Baby Dahlia" did. His wife wasn't interested in dancing for him or trying to stimulate him into a frenzy. Dahlia was fun in a way his wife couldn't be. Conn … his wife just wasn't that way. He knew now she never had been.

She had, after all, never lost the baby weight after Kevin was born. Those extra twenty pounds made her look less appealing. He concluded if she really loved him, she would have made an effort to make herself pretty for him, the way his Baby Dahlia did.

Maybe once we were happy, but we've drifted apart. We don't even have all that much in common. I love football and sports and action; she loves reading. Reading! How much fun could that be? Who would want to sit around all day with a book? And she wanted to be a writer. Imagine that? Who would want to be a boring old writer? All they do is sit around all day and make up stories. Their stories aren't even true. They make up stuff to write. In fact, you could say all they do is sit around and lie. All the time. What kind of life is that? Reading and lying.

Flip was going to move on with his life. His wife was an anchor to him. And they simply weren't happy. Not anymore. Maybe they should have a time of separation when he got home. That would probably do them some good. Maybe some time apart would make them love each other again. He knew in his heart his wife wasn't happy. And didn't she deserve to be happy too? Both of them deserved happiness, not just him. He would be doing her a favor, right? He wasn't making her happy anymore than she was making him happy. And she was a good woman. Yes, a separation was the best thing for the two of them. She deserved to experience the same happiness he had felt this week. She would thank him someday.

And besides, who wanted to live in a marriage without love? Right? God is a God of love. How pleased would God be if they weren't happy and in love? That's not a good testimony. How could he possibly tell someone about God's love if he wasn't in love with his own wife? It's impossible.

And then there are the kids to factor into this. Don't the kids deserve to have parents who are happy and in love? What an injustice to raise our kids in a loveless marriage. Right? They were totally irresponsible to try to demonstrate how "Christian marriage" was supposed to be if they weren't happy. The kids would have a warped sense of love. Shouldn't both he and Conn … his wife … be able to demonstrate to their kids how wonderful marriage is when the parents were in love?

After thinking about his life, Flip had no choice but to conclude he simply had to separate from his wife. That action was the best for everyone involved. Yes, he was sure that was what God wanted.

CHAPTER FIVE
Justin

On Monday, Justin and Connie flew home following the best week of their lives. They had no idea how far apart they had drifted by simply doing nothing. And the healings they both received in their workshops more than paid for any inconveniences they might have endured. In the days following their return, Justin sat and wrote an email to Gerald.

Mr. Alexander:

Please allow me to thank you for what you did in our lives. Had you not cared enough to confront me—well, there is no way to know just how far off track my life would have gone. I know I was heading for disaster. I might even have ended up in an affair and divorced my wife. There is absolutely no way I can ever repay you for the kindness you have shown my wife and me.

When I left on Sunday, I can genuinely say I felt closer to God than I have in a very long time. I repented of so many sins I hadn't noticed existed. My sexual sin had grown and progressed to such a degree my career was threatened; my marriage was suffering. My thoughts and even my prayers were hindered so much so I couldn't even recognize the lies I had embraced as truth.

God has brought men into my life who have been through similar struggles to show me how to truly be free from sexual sins.

With my brothers in Christ helping me, I am ready now to let go of my old pursuits, which were cheap substitutes for God.

I have made a new goal—to be the man God created me to be.

I was able to be comfortable in the "No Shame Zone," which made for a very healing environment. God used this week to help me see and understand my individual problems. God also gave me another breakthrough, which is something I've struggled with, and that was to cry. The overwhelming hurt I felt when I realized what I have put my wife through—well, I won't do that again!

My hope and prayers are not just for me but also for each and every one of my brothers in Christ and for those who have not accepted Him as their Savior. May we have the victory—though the power of Jesus—and may we continue to follow through in the years to come.

I look forward to meeting with you next week.

Once he was back at work, Justin knew he had to face James Kendall, his boss, the bank president. He knew Kendall would have much to say about his absence from the conference. Justin figured the best way to handle the situation was to simply approach him and explain his position. He arrived for work early that morning knowing Mr. Kendall would be there and others would not—they'd be able to have some privacy. He knocked on the door. "Mr. Kendall? May I have a moment?"

Kendall looked up from unenthusiastically dipping a tea bag into a cup. "Justin, come in. May I offer you a cup of tea?"

"No, thank you, sir. I'm a coffee man, myself."

Kendall scowled and indicated his cup. "My doctors have taken coffee away from me. They said I'm too acidic or I'm making too much acid or something. But my heartburn is so severe I simply can't continue suffering many more sleepless nights. I'll be an old man before my time."

The idea he wasn't already an old man made Justin smile. James Kendall had thinning gray hair that had to be combed over several times to give any appearance of volume. He was in his mid-seventies but, for the most part, he was holding up pretty well.

He fussed with his tea bag for a moment longer and then gave up and took a sip. His curled lips expressed his lack of enthusiasm for his new daily habit. "What can I do for you, Justin? How was your trip?"

"The trip was fine. Good, easy flights. It's just a long day getting from the East Coast back to here."

"How was your speech? I understand you did quite well."

Of course, he would already know! He probably had someone record the speech for him to ensure quality control. Kendall did have the reputation of the firm to protect after all. "I think my speech was a resounding success. I made some new contacts that might prove to be very profitable to us."

Kendall looked at Justin over the rim of his teacup. Something was brewing in his mind, but Justin had no way of knowing what it was. "So, you made new contacts, eh?"

"Yes, I met a man named Gerald Alexander, who introduced me to several of his associates. They seemed like they were some pretty heavy hitters at one point in the past."

Kendall mulled that over for a moment. "And what did you do with these men?"

Justin was suddenly wary. Was he even supposed to talk about the Lair? Were there rules about discussing things he knew about them? Did he actually know anything about them? Gerald never said one way or the other. If talking about them was a big deal, Gerald would have said something; he wasn't the kind of man who let things slip past him. "Well, they invited me to play golf with them the next day."

Kendall seemed to jump in his seat. He sipped his tea and smiled— as if the tea tasted better. "And did you play golf with them?"

Justin scrunched his lips. This was the part of the conversation he was not going to relish. *Best to get it over with.* "No. I had to change my plans …"

Kendall interrupted him. "And that's when you left the conference?" He sat his tea down and began to dip the bag into the cup again.

Justin should have known that Kendall was already on top of everything. He had been in the industry for a lifetime. He had contacts all over the world. "Yes, sir. I had breakfast with him, Gerald that is, the next morning and discussed the matter with him."

His eyes sparkled again and Justin was sure it wasn't the tea bag. "He invited you to have breakfast? Was anyone else there?"

"Not really. The other members were in the room, but they didn't sit with us if that's what you mean." Justin wanted to get back to his leaving the conference, but Kendall kept pressing him.

"So, the other members were close by? In the same room? Or did you see them from a distance?"

Justin was confused by this line of questioning. It wasn't as if he'd been at a Star Trek convention meeting the cast. It was a banking conference and breakfast—no more than that. "We were all in the same room. They came by our table and said good morning. That was it."

"Ah," he leaned back in his chair. "They came by your table, did they?" He snapped his fingers. "It sounds very positive."

"Uh, yes, sir. It was very positive. But I wanted to tell you I didn't attend the conference…"

"Oh, blast the conference. Who cares about a silly old conference? You had breakfast with the Lair." His voice seemed reverent.

"You know about the Lair?"

Kendall sighed deeply. "I know about it, but I don't know them myself." He pretended to stir his tea, even though there was no sugar or cream in it. "I've heard the stories, but I've never been so privileged. Please, tell me more. Who did you actually meet?"

Justin shrugged. "I met everyone who was there. I'd guess about thirty or so."

"Wonderful. Do you remember names?"

"Yes, I remember a few."

Kendall banged his tea on the table. "Well, go on and tell me, boy. Don't make me beg."

"Oh, sorry! We, Gerald and I, that is, set up a golf date with Walter Bigger, Sam Summer, Luke Dressler, and Edward Robinson …"

"Edward Robinson?" Kendall almost jumped from his chair. "Did you know he was supposed to be part of the real Knights Templar? And not the modern version, mind you. The original medieval group from the twelfth century. Of course, he's old enough to be a founding member. What did he say to you?"

Justin shook his head. "Not much. We talked a little about golf and then he said he was glad to have me on board, or something like that. Why?"

"You darn fool! You have no idea what happened or who those people are, do you?"

"I'm starting to get the idea. What do you know?"

"Nothing! That's just it. I know nothing. No one does. You meet those men by invitation only. They've been around since the first banks were founded in the Colonies. It's a small group. I'd say less than a hundred. But that's just it. No one knows how many men there are."

"And women," Justin added.

"Women, too?" Suddenly the tea seemed to taste better again. "I had no idea."

Justin laughed. "Me, neither." Maybe he had attended a Star Trek convention and met Captain Kirk himself. Or even better, Seven of Nine. "Sir? What's prompting your interest in these people?"

He sat the tea down rather abruptly. "I received a phone call from Gerald Alexander at my home on Sunday night. He told me about your speech and about meeting with you."

"Wait a minute, Gerald called you? Why?"

"He wanted to tell me you weren't going to attend the conference and he had other plans for you."

"But why would he do that?" Justin was starting to become paranoid. Who were these people?

"Justin, you just don't get it. They've been following you for several years. I've met with Gerald Alexander several times. He has come here to the office more than once. At first, I thought he was trying to recruit you, but he just wanted to hear my opinion about you as a man and an employee. He would ask questions like, "Does he work all night? Does he spend time with his family? Does he have affairs with the tellers? You know, those kinds of questions—as if they were doing a background check on you. All very secretive, mind you." He sipped his tea, which had grown cold. "Blech," he murmured. "Anyway, he said you passed the test and he wanted to start working with you, but you had some things to take care of first. Something about a workshop."

"And that was on Sunday? What time did he call?"

"At precisely nine thirty, local time. Why? Is that important?"

"Because my wife called me on the beach at … wait a minute." He looked at his cell phone. "At twelve minutes past midnight. That would be twelve after nine here." Justin sat still for a minute while his mind went into overdrive. "And he said I passed the test?"

"Yes, he was very clear about that. Why?"

Did he mean Dahlia? "And he called you at nine-thirty?"

"Asked and answered."

His mind was reeling. *Dahlia! They sent Dahlia to test me. I should have known a woman like Dahlia would never be interested in me. I'm not handsome. When a woman who looks like her pays attention to someone as ordinary as me, then beware. I'm carrying ten extra pounds myself. Maybe fifteen. There were plenty of fit, younger, more attractive men at that conference, and she chose me? I should have suspected a trap.* His next thought was, *how dare they? How dare they play games with my life? What if I'd failed that test? What if Connie hadn't called just in the nick of time? Who are these people intruding into my life?*

Kendall could tell he was agitated. "What's the matter?"

"It's just those people have no right to play games with my life. What they did to me could have destroyed me. Entirely." He ran his fingers through his hair. "And they preached about morals and upright behavior ..."

Kendall squinted and then shook his head. "You just don't get it, do you? We're not talking about Big Brother sticking his long, pointy nose into your life. This is the Lair. And they're vetting you. We're talking about a group as elite as the Bilderbergs, maybe even the Illuminati. They don't just extend an invitation because you have a winning smile. They want to know how you'll be when the rubber meets the road. And they will have their proof by fire. The kind of wealth these men manage makes our national debt a mere shadow of the mountain, so to speak. You and I both know our country is the Titanic and the iceberg is our economy. America has already hit the iceberg, it just hasn't sunk yet. We're taking on water, but we have enough bilge pumps to stay afloat. Eventually, the water will win—always does. And when that happens, someone will step up and reclaim our nation. They want to know who you are. They want to know if you have integrity … when no one is watching." Kendall was getting fired up and he was pointing at him with a stiff finger. "I demand you're proven. There's too much at stake for the rest of us. So, you can get off your high horse and reconsider just what is happening in your life."

Justin was stunned. He had no idea Kendall could be so passionate. He normally seemed like one of the premier members of the sour-faced club. Now that he was on his soapbox, his words rang true. There was more at stake than simply investing in the economy. "I wonder what being a member of this group will mean to my family. Will it be good or bad?"

Kendall considered that for a moment. "For a young man like you, family is a prime factor in your everyday life. I would imagine several candidates have been rejected because their family life was out of order. So I imagine they will want to know if your family is healthy in every regard. So, be a good father to Kevin and Ginger. Be a good husband to Connie. Be the very thing you already are."

Justin had no idea James Kendall even knew about his family. He felt humbled the Lair regarded him in such high esteem. There were so many rusty bolts that needed to be tightened in his life. He didn't take his son fishing nearly enough. He wanted to start taking his daughter on dates so he could show her how a man should treat a woman. And he wanted to continue reinforcing his wife following those life-changing workshops. He remembered she'd always wanted to write a book. He made a mental note to ask her about that.

Throughout the rest of his day, he sat bewildered. What was he supposed to do now? Was he still being tested?

The main thing he actually had to accomplish for the day was to hire a new personal assistant for his department. He'd had an incredibly gifted personal secretary before he left for the conference and she would be hard to replace. She was a very gifted researcher and she had a charm that made most people love her instantly. She and her husband had been trying to have a baby for several years, and after a few miscarriages, she wanted to stay at home where she could rest and not work during this pregnancy. She would be sorely missed.

He had interviews scheduled throughout the afternoon that would keep him occupied until the time to go home. He had so many things he needed to be doing and few of them involved his work. He remembered seeing a new fly rod at Big R. Kevin would probably enjoy having a new rod to take to Brush Lake. And he wanted to buy a gold-panning kit he'd seen. Both kids would probably enjoy doing a little prospecting along the Moyie River, or even up on Smith Creek. In fact, that would be a great family project. Connie had suggested gold panning a year or so back as a fun family outing, but he'd never gotten around to buying the equipment.

He went through the motions of interviewing secretaries without sincerely investing himself into the prospect. There were only five qualified candidates once he starting looking at the applications. Several didn't have the type of experience he needed, but he was willing to invest the effort into training the right person if someone applied who didn't quite meet the standard.

He wanted a personal assistant who was charming and confident, who could read and accurately interpret body language. Moreover, he wanted a person who could conduct the kind of research needed to make good investment decisions. He didn't want a pretty face who could only answer the phone. The position was fairly involved with research when not answering the phone or interacting with clients.

By the end of the day, he had reduced his candidates down to two women. Janet was an interesting applicant. She was the forty-year-old mother of a high school girl and was new to the area. She'd lost her husband, which necessitated her return to the workforce. Her background involved freelance work researching companies for large investment firms, but she hadn't worked in the field for more than fifteen years. When her daughter was born, she'd become a stay-at-home mom. She had a pleasant air about her and he suspected she would be skilled at reading clients' moods and body language. Her minor in college had been psychology so she had been exposed to the basic principles of human behavior.

His other candidate was a twenty-seven-year-old college graduate who'd worked as a ski instructor to pay her way through school. Mercedes had worked for Merrill Lynch as an investment analyst until recently. She'd left her previous job in Seattle because her boss had been sexually harassing her. She had a very pretty smile and had a dynamic way of interacting with others. She was a natural born leader.

The biggest differences between the two candidates were age and experience. Janet was older and wiser, but she wasn't as fit and active as Mercedes. Mercedes was dynamic, but she was apprehensive because of the EEO issues surrounding her previous job.

Justin needed to make his final decision by tomorrow. If he were truly honest with himself, he knew Janet was the right choice, but she wasn't pretty enough. Mercedes caught his eye from her blond ski bunny look to her flirty smile. Despite his progress over the last few days, he knew he still had tendencies to gravitate towards fun, exciting women. He already had decided Mercedes was his new secretary, but he was conflicted about his decision because he now recognized his weakness. He kept telling himself this was only a secretarial position. He shouldn't make too much out of filling the position one way or the other.

By the time he finished with his office duties and stumbled through the door with his new family-friendly items in tow, dinner was on the table. He found Connie in the kitchen pulling the pot roast out of the oven. "Hey, babe," she greeted him cheerfully.

"That smells good," he mentioned as he kissed her in passing.

"What's all that stuff?"

"This is a new fly rod for Kevin. I've been promising to take him fishing, and this seemed like a great place to start. His old one was a little worn, don't you think?"

"I didn't notice, but I like the idea. What's in the box?"

His smile betrayed his suppressed enthusiasm. "This is a gold-panning kit. It came with four pans, a gold extraction squeeze thing, a magnifying glass, some vials, and all the literature we need to get started."

Her approval was evident. "Cool! Maybe we can get started this weekend."

"My thoughts exactly."

"Good, now go wash up. Dinner is on the table now."

"Yes, ma'am."

"Come back here! I want another kiss."

Her thick brown hair had a few streaks of gray, but he thought they highlighted her complexion nicely. She had a soft, inviting face spattered with a few freckles. Looking at her from across the room, he thought to himself, *she still does it for me*. Those few extra pounds weren't such a big deal and kind of made her cuter. She was definitely the woman he'd fallen in love with all those years ago. The fact she wasn't a naïve college co-ed might make her more attractive now. Her maturity was a compliment to her and her age actually made her hotter than she'd been when she wore size eight pants.

She noticed him gawking at her and exclaimed, "What?"

"I'm just remembering why I married you."

She fixed a stray hair and seemed to blush. "Nice to hear," she pointed at him. "Now go wash up before my pot roast gets cold." After his prompt "yes, ma'am," she watched him disappear around the corner.

He is a changed man. It's been so long since he looked at me like that. I wonder how we drifted so far apart. We just stopped making the effort and then started drifting. We love each other, but the spark seems gone. I'm so glad we went to the Every Man's Battle and Women in the Battle workshops!

I know all married couples go through these cycles. I'm responsible too. I haven't tried to be involved in his interests. I've wrapped myself up in my books and movies. Reading about romance is very satisfying even if the books don't reflect reality. I dearly love Justin—we just needed a push to get interested in being interesting again.

But the way he was feasting his eyes on me today was exciting! I'll have to find a way to show my appreciation. Maybe a little of that perfume he likes? Some Japanese Cherry Blossom just might do the trick. Sometimes the best way to motivate Justin to action is with a little perfume and some freshly shaved legs.

"Kids," she yelled. "Time to eat." She smiled deep within her soul. Things were better than they had been in a long time.

CHAPTER SIX
Flip

His flight home from the conference was torture. He hadn't anticipated how anxious he would be returning to … her. When he'd called last night to remind her of his arrival in Spokane, she had been terse with him, which irritated him greatly. He had been very civil to her. He didn't deserve to have her treat him with disrespect. He was more convinced than ever their differences were too severe to be salvaged.

He tried not to think of Dahlia, who was flying home to her husband as well. She was fantastic. If he had married her, well, things would be different. They were so compatible. They never fought. There was nothing for them to fight about. She was interested in him, and she respected him. He found her to be exhilarating. If he had married her, life would be perfect. She adored him and would have no reason to be cross with him. Yes, he'd found the perfect woman. Except she was another man's wife. Oh well. She was almost perfect.

He stepped into the lavatory somewhere over Colorado. He paused a moment before exiting and cast a glance into the mirror. The man looking back at him seemed wiser and more interesting. He'd only needed an awakening to realize just how awesome he really was. Dahlia had drawn the man who was hidden inside of him to the surface. He was a little harder and little more masculine. He knew what he wanted and he was willing to take it.

As he made his way to his seat, he came face to face with the flight attendant, who batted her eyes at him as they squeezed past each other. He thought maybe she brushed against him more closely than she had to. She probably saw his masculine strength and didn't even realize she was drawn to him. When she was serving the mid-flight snacks, he noticed she leaned closer to him than the other passengers. And why not? He was a man who knew what he wanted. He found it a little surprising he was so comfortable with desiring another woman's attention. But, now he and … his wife, were finished, he had better start keeping his eyes open. He certainly wasn't going to be alone. Not for long. And he shouldn't have trouble finding another woman. After all, Dahlia had pointed out to him on Thursday, "You are a desirable hunk of man meat." Of course, she was wearing a leopard print negligee, but she was still adamant about his desirability. He knew he was a player, so women beware!

When he arrived at Spokane, Connie met him on the street in front of the terminals. She greeted him with a kiss and noticed when he didn't engage her. She had deliberately put on his preferred perfume, Japanese Cherry Blossom, which he always described as his favorite. He'd never failed to mention the scent when she wore it. She'd also spent some extra cash and bought a negligee he would probably enjoy.

But he was so distant. She knew something was wrong. All of her intuitions told her somehow he was different. He wouldn't look at her and his answers were short.

"Did you find any Benne Wafers when you were in South Carolina?"

"I was too busy at the conference to go looking for some stupid cookies!"

Connie was certain something was wrong. Her stomach churned and she felt an odd ache in the center of her chest.

She chided herself, *I'm being silly. He's probably just tired. The eight-hour flight here from the Carolinas is exhausting.*

Maybe he was still hurt after she accused him of being unfaithful. She'd regretted that instantly. And she knew it wasn't true. He had never strayed from her. Things might not be perfect between them, but they still had a good marriage. They were happy, even though they could be happier. One thing she could rely on was his steadfast love for her. They had always loved each other. *Yes, that has to be the problem. I've hurt him and I need to make it up to him.*

The two-hour drive home was awkward. He hardly spoke to her, but she didn't want to force him to talk.

"I missed you. I'm looking forward to spending some time with you this evening."

He seemed irritated.

"I made your favorite meal for you as a welcome home present."

"That's nice."

When they got home, Connie called the kids to come down and say hello to their father, but he greeted them with the same lackluster effort. When Connie placed piping hot lasagna on the table, he seemed bored.

After dinner, they usually sat on the patio and enjoyed the cool of the evening. Connie busied herself lighting the tiki torches lining the patio and almost dropped her lighter when Justin came out of the house carrying a drink. "What's that?"

"It's a martini," he replied sharply as if he shouldn't have to answer an obvious question.

She couldn't believe it. "When did you start drinking?"

"I had a few with the guys at the conference. Got to where I liked them, so I brought some home with me."

"Oh," she replied. *He's acting weird, but I'll play.* "Did you bring enough home for two?"

He seemed irritated, but got up and went into the house while she sat under the stars and listened to the bullbats bellowing at each other in the sky above. When he returned, he almost slapped the drink into her hands.

"Thank you."

"Yeah."

He drank his martini faster than she did and got up to get another. Connie found the drink difficult to enjoy. She'd never liked liquor. She sipped some more to give her courage to apologize for accusing him of an affair. For some reason, she simply couldn't come out and say it. She gritted her teeth and swallowed the martini, coughing.

When Flip returned with his second, even larger drink, he was already slightly intoxicated.

Meanwhile, Connie had mustered the strength to make her formal apology. "Justin," she began. "I'm so sorry I accused you of being unfaithful to me the other day. I know you better than that. I know you never cheated on me. Please forgive me for being so ugly to you."

Her act of contrition made him grimace. "Apology accepted," he slurred out.

"Justin?"

"Hmm?"

"Are you listening to me?"

"What?"

"I asked if you would forgive me for accusing you of having an affair."

"Justin?" He still hadn't responded to her and she said his name sharply.

"Sorry." He sat his now empty tumbler on the table next to him. "I've gotten so used to being called Flip again I hardly noticed you calling me."

"Flip? When have you ever gone by Flip? That's a nickname you've never really liked."

"Norm started it up at the conference. He called me Flip on stage, and from then on, I was known as Flip. Those guys probably don't even know my real name." He shrugged. "I dunno, I kind of like it. Seems more masculine than Justin."

She shook her head in disbelief. "Flip seems more masculine? It makes you seem like a goofy college kid if anything."

"What bee got into your bonnet?"

"Well, nothing, really. It's just you never liked Flip and now you've come home to a new identity. You aren't acting the same as when you left. Something is off about you. I'm wondering what changed?"

"Me? I've changed? What about you? All I've had since I've been home is you hounding me and treating me like a child. I don't need you riding me all the time, that's for sure."

She was shocked. "What? What are you talking about? I've been riding you? If anything, I've been very pleasant."

"From where I'm sitting you have been very accusatory."

"Accusatory?" She couldn't believe her ears. She could feel her anger rising. "Are you kidding me? What have I accused you of?"

"You said something about an affair." His voice was strained.

"No, what I said was I knew you weren't having an affair."

"Well, if I have, it's your fault."

"You've got to be kidding!" Had he lost his mind completely? "How could that possibly be my fault?"

"You know we aren't happy," he stammered.

"Maybe there were some things we could do differently, but I'm not unhappy."

He shook his head. "Oh, no, you don't. If you were honest, you would admit you aren't happy. Just like I'm willing to admit I'm not happy."

"What?" She wanted to scream. "What do you mean, you aren't happy?"

"It's true. I haven't been happy in a long time. It's a fact. And you know it."

"What I know is you don't need to drink any more martinis. Something's wrong with you. Now tell me what it is. Tell me why we're fighting."

He was silent.

"Great. Just great. I spent all week regretting how I hurt you with that stupid question. All night I've tried to apologize to you. And now … and now …" Tears sprang to her eyes.

"Now what's the matter?" he jumped at her. "First you accuse me of adultery and then you get mad and start crying. What a happy home for me to come to. It's no wonder I thought about not coming back at all."

His words sent a chill down her spine. "You thought about not coming back?" She felt like she was about to lose her mind. "Why?"

"Because we aren't happy anymore. We aren't in love anymore. And we haven't been in a long time."

"That's news to me, Buster. When I woke up this morning, I was happy and in love. What happened to you?"

He dismissed her. "You know that's not true. We haven't been happy in a long time. Maybe at first, but not anymore."

She was exasperated. "No, that's not true. Until about five minutes ago, I was perfectly happy. And now, well, the whole world seems to be falling apart. What's going on, Justin?"

"I told you, I prefer Flip."

"Well, pound sand, Flip! Tell me why you're acting like you're on drugs."

"I want to talk to you, but you're being argumentative."

Connie felt lost. *What's happening? One martini and I'm in the Twilight Zone.* "Justin, let's just back up for a minute. Something's clearly wrong. I have no idea what it is. Please tell me what's wrong."

"I think we need to separate for a while," he managed to say after a moment.

She couldn't believe her ears. "We need to separate? Is that what you said?"

"Yes. I think it's for the best. I can't live like this anymore."

"And why do you think we should separate?"

"Because I realized we don't love each other anymore, and I think you would admit it if you would just be honest."

Connie stared at him with bewildered eyes. *Is he on drugs? Something has to be causing this irrational behavior.* There was only one explanation she could think of that made any sense. She exhaled in preparation and then asked the question. "Are you having an affair?"

He slept in the guest room that night after he refused to talk to Connie about his week with Dahlia.

She hadn't gotten him to confess he was involved, but she seemed absolutely certain he was, which just went to prove she was a horrible person. She would simply assume the worst without ever hearing him say it. If he denied the liaison, then she had no proof to accuse him of infidelity. She was convicting him without evidence. It was categorically unfair.

Since he had so much trouble sleeping, he went to work early and found himself dodging Old Man Kendall for most of the morning. Kendall was extraordinarily grumpy and kept fussing about wanting coffee. *Why doesn't the old man just go and get some coffee if it's that important?*

When Kendall finally cornered him in the break room just before lunch, Flip felt pinned down and hard-pressed to account for his time away.

"I heard that your speech went well. What did you think?"

Flip shrugged. "I was happy with it. I made several new contacts following the speech and even managed to set up a golf game with a few old timers who were too old to golf properly."

"Is that a fact? I understood you didn't actually make it to your tee time."

Flip shrugged. "I ended up being delayed at the conference and didn't get there in time. I decided it would be better to catch the group another day."

"So," the old man asked. "How was the rest of the conference?"

"It was just like any conference. Boring is boring. It's hard to sit in a room with a bunch of boring lectures lined up day after day."

"Is that why you ditched most of the conference?"

"Oh, that's not true. I did abandon some of the morning sessions, but I attended the important stuff."

"Well, Mr. Grey," Kendall got close to his face and pressed in. "I'll have you know I don't pay for you to attend those conferences so you can play footsie with a hooker all week. Your behavior is an embarrassment to our employees, our clients, and this town. Not to mention what your wife must think. Of course, I'm assuming you're man enough to admit to her you were fishing in another man's pond all week while she was at home cleaning your house and cooking for your children."

Kendall pointed at Connie across the lobby at her teller desk. "That is a precious woman, Grey. She has stood by you through it all. She doesn't deserve to be treated as your seconds. If I were twenty years younger, I would ask her out myself. Now get your act together. If I see you pull another stunt like that again, it will be your job. Are we clear?"

Flip had enough sense to allow the old man to vent his anger and followed his final question with a smug, "Yes, sir."

"Unfortunately, you will never know just what you just tossed away this week. I happen to know Gerald Alexander. I talked to him on the phone Monday morning. He said he had withdrawn your name from membership with the Lair." Kendall frowned and then looked as if he could spit at him. "What a putz. You traded a membership in the Lair for a hooker with big headlights. Talk about trading your birthright for a bowl of grits. Now get back to work before I fire you."

Flip slunk away grateful no one else heard the thrashing he had just endured. *How could Kendall have known about Dahlia? And the nerve he has to call her a hooker. Why, if he were a few years younger, I would have set the record straight, and it would have happened out in the parking lot, where real men settle their issues.*

A few minutes later, he found himself trying to apply salve to his wounded soul by visiting his porn site with his smartphone. The women he viewed reminded him of Baby Dahlia, his one true love. The only person who knew who he really was and appreciated him for who he was. He didn't have to pretend with her, he could just be himself. He dearly wished he could be with her again, to walk with her on the beach knowing they wore only their robes. Or to have her feed him strawberries after their morning liaison.

When he finally got back to work, he had interviews to conduct to replace the secretary for his department. His previous girl had had a baby and turned in her resignation. She'd been a highly valued employee. *The guy who managed to father that baby sure was lucky. She was a sight for sore eyes! Too bad she spoiled such a beautiful figure by having a baby. Yeah, it'll be hard to find an equal to her.*

Most of the afternoon he spent weeding out the applicants and trying to find the right person for the job. Finally, after a full day of interviews, he had only one qualified applicant remaining. Her name was Mercedes. She had ample experience and was very charming. She was well-defined for the job.

Flip never tried to hide he was staring at her, practically undressing her with his eyes. She had to know she had a good shot at getting hired. Flip watched her run into the restroom before her interview. When she came out, she'd changed into a low-cut blouse, which she must have kept in her purse. She laughed and flirted and adjusted her amenities until she had him eating out of her hand. Who knows? Maybe they could become better friends in the future?

Going home that evening was difficult. Connie was still on the warpath about his activities while at the conference. He had yet to admit anything had happened. *A real man doesn't stand for a woman's nosing in his affairs. A real man doesn't get henpecked. That woman can pound sand as far as I'm concerned.*

Connie gave him the cold, silent treatment most of the evening. She was moody and seemed to be crying quite a bit. *Just more evidence we're not really in love.*

Oh well, she could be difficult if she wanted. He looked forward to helping Mercedes with her orientation tomorrow. She kind of reminded him of his beloved Dahlia.

CHAPTER SEVEN
Justin

The Greys found a great place to undertake all of their new hobbies at the same time. After reading his book on how to gold pan, he remembered a place near where Smith Creek emptied into the Kootenai River and had left behind a massive sand bar that had to be full of gold. And it was close to the road, which was even better. They made a day of it, taking everything they would need for roasting hotdogs and marshmallows and eating watermelon. The kids put on their swimsuits and splashed in the shallow, cold water of Smith Creek. And what a beautiful day for their outing too. The sun was high in the sky with not a cloud in sight, and the temperature pegged at 73 degrees. Pines trees and soaring eagles surrounded them as well as majestic snowcapped mountains. Could life be any better?

Kevin was excited to use his new fly rod, but the gold pans looked more fun for the moment. They dug sand out of the creek and washed it down in their pans for several minutes before Connie exclaimed, "Holy wow! This water is freezing!"

"Girls are such sissies," Kevin laughed.

"Watch it, Buster. I was in labor with you for thirteen hours."

Justin glanced at Connie, "It was more like seventeen hours."

Connie nodded. "Yes, I think you're right. It was every bit of twenty hours. So, no calling us girls sissies just because we like warm water."

Kevin looked up from his pan and asked, "Is that why they always send the husband after warm water and towels?"

Justin wasn't sure if Kevin missed the joke or made one of his own, but he no longer cared. "Look at this! I see gold!"

Everyone rushed to squeeze around him. "Where," "I can't see it," and "Are you sure?"

"See that?" he pointed.

"Do you mean that tiny speck of something?" Kevin asked.

"Aw, it's so cute! We found a teensy, tiny sparkle in the river."

"Get me that squeezy thing from the kit."

"Does Parker use one of those on Gold Rush?"

Justin frowned. "Parker doesn't need one of these on Gold Rush. He uses a shovel."

Connie patted him on the hand once he had his speck suctioned into the tube. "We will never starve as long as we have you. Now," she stood and stretched. "I'm going to find a cup of hot coffee and sit in the sun."

Ginger decided she would rather catch frogs on the edge of the water and started chasing them, even catching a few of the unlucky ones.

After Justin had built a fire and they roasted their hotdogs and finished off the marshmallows, he and Kevin focused on fishing and began casting their lines in the massive Kootenai River.

"Gosh, Dad! Where are all the fish?"

I don't know, Kevin—ooh look! You've got a bite!"

"I caught a rainbow trout! Can we keep it? Will you cook it? I'll even give Ginger a taste.

Ginger, a picky eater, tried the trout but didn't care for it. *She'll probably never be a fish eater,* Justin thought.

"C'mon, Ginger, let's go see if we can find a moose," Kevin yelled to his sister.

Justin and Connie leaned back in their folding chairs and basked in the warm sunlight and the soft splashing of Smith Creek. After a few minutes of dozing in the sunlight, Connie shed her T-shirt to get a little color on her skin. Kevin didn't notice her movements at first, but when he opened his eyes and saw her wearing a bikini top, he was surprised. "Wow, where did you get that swimsuit?"

She sipped from her water bottle. "Like it? I found it at Larson's Department Store when I went to the post office the other day."

"So you went to the post office and came back with a bikini? How does that happen?"

"I could see their sidewalk sale when I mailed that box and I stopped for a look. Do you like it?"

"Do I like it? Mama, you're one hot firecracker! You're starting to look like you did in college. Only…"

"Only what?"

"Only you can't wear that in public."

She smiled at him. "And why not?"

"Because. Look at you, you'd outshine all the women and you'd have to brush off all the men. I won't have it. I prefer my women to be modest, not flaunting."

"Relax. I only bought this for sunbathing. Besides, when do we go places where I could wear a bikini?"

"Sometimes we go the Lake Pend Oreille and hang out at the beach."

She rolled her eyes at him. "Yeah, once a year we do that. When we have our summer office party. What a great time that is!" she scoffed.

"Now, Connie. There's nothing like seeing Mr. Kendall strutting his stuff."

Connie laughed. "He may not be overweight, but his trunks are sure tight."

"That's because they're 34s. He should wear a 36."

Connie dug deeper. "And hearing Melanie's stories about how awesome her kids are. Good times."

"I know, right? Last year she tried to convince me her son had skied the entire length of Pend Oreille. I didn't argue with her, but I know that's not possible."

"So how long would that be?" Connie asked.

He thought for a minute. "Hmm, let's see. There're about forty-five miles of shoreline. I think the lake has a hundred and fifty miles of surface area."

"So, there's no way that kid skied forty-five miles in one day."

"No, she said forty-five miles without stopping."

Connie sighed deeply. "I wish our kids were that awesome. Ours are only average."

Justin leaned back in his chair. "Well, just so you know you can't wear that swimsuit to the beach."

She pouted. "But what if I want Kendall to notice me? How will I get my next promotion?" she asked sarcastically

"You just have to do it on merit," he said flatly, but with a grin on his face.

"Great," she moaned. "I'll be stuck as a teller for the rest of my life."

"If you want to take the fast track, you do know a vice president who is willing to sleep with you."

She sipped from her bottle. "I've heard he's not very good in bed."

"Ha."

"Ha is right. I bet he's nothing compared to Mr. Kendall." The conversation sagged and she started thinking. "I wonder if there's any way I could go to part-time work."

"Part time? Why would you do that? The only reason you work now is so we can pay off our mortgage early."

"I'm also trying to get all my Social Security credits."

"Yep, there's a nest egg we don't want to miss out on." He glanced at her. "Do you really want to work part time?"

"I was thinking about it. Do you remember how Pastor Harris wanted a volunteer to head up that new program to help battered women?"

"What about it?"

She adjusted her chair to better catch the light. "I'm interested in helping out. Do you remember when Sandy showed up for work and she wore that huge scarf for a week?"

"Sandy? Who?"

She blinked at him. "Sandy Simpson? The redhead who left the bank a year or so back? Does that ring a bell?"

"Ah, yes, I do remember her. She was the one who sort of disappeared one day. What about the scar?"

"Not a scar. A scarf. She wore a scarf because her husband beat her. I kept trying to get her to report the abuse to the police, but she was too scared. And then she disappeared. She turned in her resignation and left, never to be seen again."

"What happened to her?"

She shrugged. "No one knows. I'd heard she moved back to Seattle to be with her mother."

"Wait a minute, she was married to Ben Simpson, right? The manager of Davis Farm Implements?"

"That's right. Why?"

"I looked into buying that place for a client. He wanted to open up some kind of rec center for kids. The place is right there by the school and probably would have worked. But Mr. Davis wouldn't sell. I dealt with Ben quite a bit."

"And?"

He shrugged. "I dunno. He didn't seem like a wife beater to me. He was an okay guy."

"They come in all forms." She redirected the conversation. "Anyway, I was thinking about scaling back my hours and volunteering with that ministry. What do you think?"

"I've never asked you to work. Working was always your choice. I always thought you wanted to get out of the house more than you wanted to pay off the mortgage quickly. So, if you want to scale back or quit altogether, it's okay with me."

The next few weeks were odd at the bank after Connie reduced her hours to twenty a week. She was a popular person at work—she was constantly tossing around her dry sense of humor and keen observations about how she saw things. Justin missed not sharing his lunch with her and he felt hollow whenever he would look over at the teller counter and she wasn't there.

Mercedes had proven to be a capital secretary. She was quick and efficient and was always flashing a bright, toothy smile. The clients liked her and Mr. Kendall was proud to spend time helping her learn the job. He was, after all, a hands-on kind of boss.

Her smart business outfits caused quite a stir with the tellers, who immediately concluded she intended to use all her skills to get ahead in the business. Her clothes definitely complimented her finer features, accentuating the positive at every curve. The women didn't trust her and the men thought she was wonderful.

Justin noticed that many eyes were watching her closely when the women perceived Mercedes was paying close attention to him now Connie had reduced her hours and wasn't there to observe what was going on. He could see they noticed how Mercedes would lean closer to him and would often stretch whenever he was walking past her. She loved to flip her hair and laugh gaily when talking to him at his desk.

They seemed to think it curious that Justin seemed to be unaware of Mercedes' efforts to gain his approval. He'd known the women had always considered him to be a bit of a flirt, but he didn't troll anymore. He wasn't quite as flirty as he had been previously—he had become a different man. The question was, though, what would he do if Mercedes tried to make him her next conquest? She would be a very tempting offer to any man. The next few weeks would prove interesting indeed.

CHAPTER EIGHT
Flip

Connie pinned Flip down one day after work and made him answer her questions. She couldn't begin the healing process unless she knew what the problem was. She began with a prepared speech.

"Flip, sit down. We need to talk." She didn't have to tell him to let her talk without interruption because he hardly spoke to her anymore. "I know something is up, and I want you to explain to me what it is. I think you've found another woman. Maybe something happened at the conference. Maybe it didn't. But as your wife, I deserve to know what's going on. So, tell me now."

At first, he only scowled at her. But when she refused to relent, he confessed.

"There was another woman," he muttered. "And before you start crying," he said dismissively, "you need to know she means nothing to me. I don't intend on seeing her again. Ever. It was a one-time event."

She was so mad and heartbroken at the same time she didn't know how to respond. She wanted to cry, but for some reason the tears didn't come. Something inside of her was breaking, almost as if from the brokenness she was becoming a different woman.

"What was her name?" she demanded.

"Dahlia."

Her hands were on her hips and her eyes squeezed tightly shut. "And how many times did you …um …?"

"Just that one time," he said looking away.

"Right. Just once." She didn't buy it. "And I suppose it was the night I called to apologize for accusing you of doing that very thing?"

"If it makes you feel any better, nothing had ever happened up to that point. I have always been faithful until that night."

"Oh, yeah. That makes me feel just swell. In fact, I might just go dancing to celebrate how good that makes me feel."

"Connie, don't—"

"Don't what, Flip? Don't be critical? Don't be difficult? Don't make you feel remorse for your betrayal? What is it, Flip, that you don't want me to do? Not get mad at you? Not feel hurt?"

He was silent.

"Was she pretty?" Connie asked with a measure of regret. She wanted to know, but then again, maybe she didn't want to know. Maybe that would be another question that he refused to answer.

"Yes, she was very pretty."

She thought for a long moment before asking, "Do you regret it?"

He hung his head and stared at his shoes. "What I did was wrong. I shouldn't have done it. And I won't do it again."

"What a relief," she said dryly. "Now what?"

"Now what, what?"

"Don't make this more difficult than it has to be, Flip. Now what happens? You were the one who did this to our family. What are you going to do to fix it?"

"I just assumed we were going to separate. Is that what you want?"

"What I want is to continue to believe my husband loves me enough to stay true to me. But now I will have to settle for something less than that. You know I don't believe in divorce, even though I believe you have given me Biblical grounds. However, I'm willing to try and work things out for the sake of the kids."

"Then for the kid's sake, I will stay and try to see if we can work this out," he replied dully.

"Well, try and contain your enthusiasm. For a moment I thought the dead were going to rise from all your excitement." She shook her head. "I can tell you this, Flip. You will be the one to explain to the kids what you've done when the time is right. You need to at least appear to regret what you've done. I think you don't regret any of it. I think you were hoping you could shack up with a trollop and then come back to me as if it never happened. You were just going to take a hiatus from our marriage while you sowed some wild oats and then crawl back into my bed and spread whatever disease you picked up to me. Well, Buster, that isn't going to happen. Because it will be a long dry spell before you touch me again. You can take that to the bank." Finally, the dam broke and her tears began to flood her cheeks.

Flip did feel bad about hurting Connie. She was a good person and didn't deserve to be hurt by him or anyone else. For the most part he was confused by the fact he was sorry he hurt Connie, but he didn't regret what he did. He and Dahlia had had a great week together. It was a once in a lifetime opportunity for him and he was glad he finally experienced what true love was. Really, the only side effect he noticed was his casual indifference to Connie. She was no longer attractive to him and he even resented her for being so plain. He was also angry at himself for not realizing he was a player and he could have scored a total babe from the very first. He felt as though he'd wasted his best years on Connie when he could have been living large with some quality women.

If she wanted to try and stay together for the kids' sake, then he was willing to do so. Besides, he didn't have anywhere to go. Finding another place to live would cost him more money.

Their circumstances at work were difficult as well. Everyone knew something was going on, and it didn't take much of a rocket scientist to conclude he'd had a fling at the conference. He did feel bad Connie was being gossiped about at work because of what he had done, but it couldn't be helped.

He kept thinking Connie was watching him everywhere he went in the bank, especially when he was standing close to Mercedes. Mercedes was the only woman who didn't seem to be mad at him and he appreciated her open mind. Several times during the week, they sat together in the break room and quietly chatted about things that had nothing to do with him or Connie. She was more like a sympathetic friend who was concerned about him on a personal level. He had to admit he was enjoying having a female friend with whom he didn't share any sexual tension. They had a very pure friendship and he was glad he could relax around her without thinking about her in that way. Of course, under normal circumstances, he would have found her to be very attractive, but now he had real world experience, no one quite compared to Dahlia.

Connie, on the other hand, seethed continually about his endless stream of attention to the blond bimbo who was dressed to kill. Her shameless and constant flirting made life very difficult for Connie at work. She hated the pitying looks she got from her coworkers who all assumed what happened between her and Flip was his inability to keep his pants on at the conference. She knew they were the topic of discussion around the break table, but she didn't know what could be done about it.

The shame he'd brought upon them was stifling and the damage was permanent. Some people might be cavalier in their declaration of "who cares what others think?" Those people had never been smeared by a scandal that left their children ashamed, their families embarrassed, and their emotional health shattered.

I'm tired of feeling like I have to apologize to everyone for what Flip has done. What will my future be? Nothing good can come from this situation.

Thank goodness we don't drive to work together. I couldn't stand to be in the car with him for the commute. Besides these migraines are getting me down. Thank goodness I can just go home to my meds and my dark room when I need to.

On Friday, Connie was suffering a significant migraine and left early to take a pain pill and nausea medicine, which usually knocked her out until morning. *I'm so glad the kids have sleepovers at their friend's houses and that Flip won't be home early. I can just go to bed and try to sleep.*

The tellers had closed the windows and were making their way out of the building while Flip and Mercedes finished researching some investment figures for their late appointment. They were the last people in the bank when their appointment called to say he was having car trouble and would have to cancel the meeting.

Mercedes had not yet found herself alone with Flip and she knew he was always stripping her with his eyes. *Time to make my move. If I try to make oversized copies on the copy machine, it will jam. I only need to change a few settings. There, that should do it.* Now, she only had to get Flip to make a copy and she would take it from there.

Flip closed his office door and made his way to her desk. "Looks like you'll make it home early tonight."

"Yes, it does," she replied with a wide smile. "Big plans?"

"Who, me? I never have any plans. This is my life right here. What you see is what you get. How about you? Do you have a hot date planned?"

Mercedes flipped her hair. "I don't have anything planned. I like to play it by ear. You never know what might pop up."

"Well," he began, apparently stalling. "Do we have everything wrapped up yet?"

"Almost. I need to make a copy of this chart and send an email. Another five minutes and I can go home." She looked up at him. "Or maybe go grab a bite to eat." She held the chart in her hands.

"Hey, let me make that copy for you and you can get out of here in only two minutes."

She shrugged casually. "I don't want to put you out. I know you need to get home."

"I have nothing to get home to anymore." He pulled the chart from her hands and tried to make a copy. "Hey, this machine jammed. Do you know how to fix it?"

She rolled her eyes and complained, "Men. What good are they?" She joined him at the copy machine and when he tried to step out of the way, she motioned for him to stay put. "No, you need to know how to do this. Now pull open that panel. Okay, now pull open that panel. Good. See the jammed paper underneath that roller?"

"Where? I can't see anything."

Bingo! That's my cue. She leaned over him and pressed into his back and reached around him. She practically gave him a bear hug. "Roll that bar forward. See? There it is." She pressed against him harder and reached for the lodged paper. "You have to be careful not to rip it. Now, we've fixed your problem. Is there anything else I can do for you?"

She had him pinned against the machine and he had nowhere to go. He looked over his shoulder and into a face full of hair. He could smell her perfume. Was that Chanel? Seemed familiar. "Looks like I have no way out," he said casually.

"Is there somewhere you want to go?" she asked in a husky whisper.

"How about your place?"

CHAPTER NINE
Justin

Ginger and Justin were on a daddy-daughter dinner date at Under the Sun. Ginger knew exactly what she wanted to eat when the cute, bubbly waitress came to take their order.

"I want the Panini special and the soup."

"Do you want a half sandwich?"

"No, I'll take the other half home."

"Yum!" She turned to Justin. "And what can I get you?"

"I'll have the Reuben. But I want the half sandwich and the soup."

She wrote it down. "Those Reubens are great, but they don't reheat very well, huh? So what are you two doing today?"

He winked at Ginger. "I'm taking my daughter out on a date."

"Oh, how fun! That's so cute! I'll get those sandwiches out as soon as I can. It's starting to get busy in here."

Justin wasn't worried. "Take your time. We aren't in a rush." When she was gone to another table, he said, "Wow, she sure has a lot of, like, energy, huh?"

"She's always like that."

"And did you see how she was dressed? I really like her outfit. It's very modest, but it also makes her look very smart. When I see a girl dressed like her, I always think she must be a winner. She knows she's pretty, but doesn't try to make her beauty the focus of who she is."

"Yeah, her outfit is cute," she said while sipping her Coke.

"She reminds me of you."

"Really?" Ginger craned her neck to see the waitress better.

"See? She's very outgoing and personable. She's graceful and fun and smart. And she's respectful of others. Those are all things I like about you." He looked at her with love in his heart. Oh, how she had changed his life. There was no way he would miss one minute of her growing up. "So, you'll be in the youth group next year?"

"Uh huh."

"Are you excited about it?"

"Yes, sir. Did you know they have a drama team? They do plays and stuff and they sometimes travel to other places and do plays."

"That sounds pretty neat. Is that something you want to help with?"

"I do."

"Well, I'll bet you're the best little actor in the troop. My money is on you, darling."

"Daddy, I will be an actress, not an actor. Actors are boys."

"And you're not a boy. Is that what you're telling me?"

"Daddy! You know I'm not a boy."

"I know that. And do you know why I know that? Because you're as pretty as your momma, and she ain't no boy. There's nothing boyish about her."

They went on like that for the rest of their meal. He spent time telling her how boys should treat her, even though she still found boys to be more irritating than interesting. And he talked to her about going to college and offered a few ideas for her to consider.

When they finished their meal, they went for a hike to Snow Creek Falls, one of the most impressive falls near Bonners Ferry.

"Listen, Dad! You can already hear the water and we're not even close!"

"You're right—do you feel that temperature drop? What a relief! We should have brought our rain gear—this mist from the falls is gonna soak us."

They only paused a moment before pressing on to get away from the mist.

"Look, Ginger—see all this moss? The mist from the waterfall keeps the banks damp. That's a perfect growing environment for the moss."

On their way back to the car, Justin turned to her. "Hey? How about we go to Super One for an ice cream cone. You know you love them!"

While they sat in the charming dining area, Justin couldn't help but think about how limited the availability was for ice cream in Bonners Ferry.

That evening he sat on the patio with Connie and slapped at the occasional mosquito. He built a fire that seemed more interested in smoking rather than burning, so he kept poking the logs with a stick. They were sipping iced tea and watching the stars popping out between the clouds.

"It's a bit chilly tonight," Connie offered. "And it feels rainy. Try and get your fire stirred up."

"Working on it now." He managed to turn the smoking log over and a flame caught. "That's better."

"So, how was your date with Ginger?"

"We had fun. Our waitress was one of your biggest fans. She said you helped her sister at the hospital the other day."

"They are both sweet girls, and they come from a good family. Well, a good mom. I don't think dad is in the picture. Her sister just married wrong. It's as simple as that."

"Guess who I saw at Under the Sun when we were eating?"

"Mickey Mouse."

"Not close, but a good guess nonetheless. Mercedes was there."

"Alone?"

"Yes. She looked like she was out hiking or something for the day."

Connie thought for a minute as she stared into the fire. "I think she's into bicycles."

"She seemed very lonely. She was certainly watching us closely."

"You keep your eyes on that girl. I think she's trouble. She reminds me of a pouty cheerleader who always gets what she wants and knows what she needs to do to get it. She has a lot of ambition and is probably misguided." The fire popped and shot sparks at her legs. "Just don't ever put yourself in a position to be alone with her." Justin frowned when she said that and she caught his expression. "I'm just telling you what I see in her. She's dangerous. And yes. I trust you. I'm certain you have zero interest in her." She watched her husband smirk knowingly at her. "As a wife, I had to say it."

He wasn't offended. "Message received. I promise not to interact with her unless necessary. Scout's honor." He held up three fingers, a token of his Boy Scout days. He was contemplative for a moment. "I wonder if I should have hired Janet instead." When Connie looked confused, he clarified, "You know, that other woman?"

"Could've, would've, should've. We'll never know, and you can't play that game. She was a single mom, right? She probably would have had trouble staying late on the days you have late appointments. Only God knows." She leaned to the side to avoid a sudden uprising of smoke. "And how was Snow Creek?"

"Oh, it was magnificent. The snow is melting just right this year and the water might be even higher than last year. I wish you could have joined us."

"No, you and Ginger need time together. I'm glad you're able to do it. She really needs your input right now. She's almost a teenager, you know."

"Don't remind me. After the falls, we went to Super One and got ice cream. They have really good soft serve there."

"And cheap. It's only twenty-five cents for a huge cone." If anything, Connie was frugal. "You have to pay a full dollar at Three Mile for a cone."

"That made me think."

"Oh, brother," she rolled her eyes playfully.

"You know what this town needs?"

"Yes. A Costco."

"True enough. But I was thinking a little smaller. We could use a Baskin-Robbins and their thirty-one flavors of ice cream."

"Or a Dairy Queen. I love their ice cream."

"That would be great, too. But they're soft-serve. I'm talking about regular old ice cream you have to scoop and serve in a cup, or a cone."

"Mmmm. A waffle cone for me, please."

He wasn't finished yet. "And they're expanding right now. You can buy a franchise at a good price. About one hundred and twenty-five thousand to get started."

Connie drained the rest of her tea. "You know what I want? I want a Famous Dave's BBQ. That would be awesome. We have to drive all the way to Kalispell to get Famous Dave's. I find that to be totally unacceptable. Or what about a Macaroni Grill, or even an Olive Garden? Those are great restaurants."

He thought about it while she went into the house to replenish their teas. Those weren't bad ideas, either. The restaurants they had in Bonners Ferry were good, but there wasn't a lot of variety. The best places in town were small sports bars. He really liked Mugsy's and the Brewery, but they were both essentially the same thing. The other places were small diners. The town needed some variety.

Connie returned with their teas and a plate of fresh strawberries. "I'll tell you what we need—fast food. The only choices we have are deli sandwiches or Zip's. We could use an Arby's, MacDonald's, Burger King, or Long John Silver's. You know, one of those would be awesome."

"I'd kill for a Papa John's pizza right about now."

She moaned in desire. "Wouldn't that be awesome? If you want an investment, fast food is where it's at. We need something easy to pick up and take home. This town is ripe for some new choices. Especially family friendly choices. We never go to the casino to eat, and we're not the only ones who feel that way."

"And with new choices, come new opportunities." He threw a strawberry stem into the fire. "I'm going to start looking into those options."

"Who's your new client?"

"You."

"Me? I thought you had a real client on board. You got my hopes up for nothing. Thanks a lot, Buster."

He spent the next week researching franchises for all the restaurants they'd discussed and began to put together a proposal. Finally, after crunching numbers and collecting the information Mercedes chased down, he had an intriguing plan. On Friday, he and Mercedes finished the day by finalizing the last details. They were the last two people working and he hardly noticed it was almost six-thirty. When he did, he told her, "I'm sorry. I didn't realize it was so late. Why don't you clock out? I'm sure you have better things to do than hang out here on a Friday night."

"Oh, I don't mind. Besides, I don't want to leave the rest of it for you to do." Her answer seemed genuine.

"Nonsense. A young woman should be out on a date, not hanging out with her boss at a bank. Now shut down and go enjoy your weekend."

"Really, Justin." It was the first time she addressed him by his first name. "I enjoy helping you with these projects. You have a fascinating mind and I love to see you in action."

"Ah, well." *Sure didn't take long for this conversation to become awkward.* "We're about finished with this project. I'm certain it's ready to go. So, thank you anyway."

Mercedes shrugged and look into his eyes. "I'm still pretty new to town. I don't have anywhere to go. You know what sounds good? The Hydra Steakhouse in Sandpoint and a big, juicy, steak." She smiled warmly. "I get kind of lonely around here; I live alone, you know." She started curling a strand of hair around her finger.

"No, I didn't know that." *I need to stop this discussion before something bad happens.* "I haven't spent any time thinking about your living arrangements. Besides, I'm sure Connie wouldn't appreciate me thinking about you, anyway."

Mercedes shrunk. "Of course. I didn't mean anything by it. I was just talking. I don't really have anyone to talk to around here." She looked as though she were about to cry, which pushed one of his buttons. He was a very compassionate man.

"Well, I have to get home. Connie will have dinner ready by now."

"Have a good weekend." She feigned a cheerful goodbye.

"Bye, now." He went back into his office and appeared to be on the phone until she clocked out and left. *Wow, that could have been bad. Thank God Connie thought to warn me about her. I might have walked right into that ambush without realizing what was happening. And Mercedes is a tempting woman. She would be a difficult woman to turn down for a man who didn't have principles or who was weak. I must admit I'm a bit flattered by the attention. Nice to know I still have some game.* But that was a door he didn't want to open. Nothing good would ever come from having an affair, no matter how appealing the offer seemed. There was no way he could anticipate just how many people and things a mistake like that would affect. One mistake like that could negatively change every person he knew.

The first thing he needed to do was let Connie know what happened. She was one of his biggest defenses. Staying accountable to her was paramount to keeping their relationship healthy. It would also strengthen her trust in him.

The next thing he needed to do was to send an email to Gerald, who had become something of an accountability partner for him. Gerald wasn't shy about asking him difficult questions such as, "have you been exposed to pornography this week? Or have you had a fight with your wife this week?" At first his questions seemed intrusive, but he had to admit he was very careful about the things he did and thought about knowing Gerald was going to ask. No man was above being accountable for everything he does. No man.

"Are you mad? Absolutely not." James Kendall was adamant. "Have you fallen off your rocker? There is no way on earth Bonners Ferry could support this kind of enterprise. One fast food restaurant, maybe. But three? You're out of your ever-loving mind."

Justin wasn't ready to give up. "Look at this column of numbers. Do you see how many people in Bonners Ferry drive to Sandpoint just to eat something different? That's money which could be spent in Bonners."

"And while they're at Sandpoint, they go to Wal-Mart. And to the mall for a movie."

"True. But once Super One opened in Bonners, many people quit going to Wal-Mart unless they were already in Sandpoint. They're satisfied not to spend the gas money to drive thirty miles when they can get the same thing here for almost the same price. Super One made this venture possible."

"I don't know," Kendall was a stubborn man. "There's just not enough population to support that much industry."

"And that's where you're wrong. There are so many Canadians who drive through Bonners Ferry every day. A lot of them drive to Sandpoint or Coeur d'Alene to do their shopping. And then they drive right back through Bonners Ferry. Think about it. You can get them coming, and then going."

He put another piece of paper in front of him. "And Highway 2 is a major tourist route. It's the only way to get to Montana unless you drive all the way down to Sandpoint and catch Highway 200, which doesn't go through many towns. At least Highway 2 takes you to Kalispell and to Glacier National Park. I'm telling you. The money is in Bonners Ferry; it's a gold mine."

"But you would have to buy property and then build three brand new buildings. That's the bulk of your expenses right there. No, you can't sustain the cash flow to get past the initial investment and make a profit. It just can't be done."

"But have I ever suggested a bad investment?"

Kendall pursed his lips together. "Not until today." He shook his head. "I'm sorry. The answer is no. And that's final."

CHAPTER TEN
Flip

He was certain Connie knew about his evening with Mercedes. She hadn't said anything, but she was a very intuitive woman. How could she not know? She had gone home with a migraine and took some pills that put her to sleep until mid-Saturday morning. He was back home by three a.m., but she was a woman. And women knew things like that.

Mercedes proved to be fun. She knew lots of things; she wasn't innocent in that regard. But, she still wasn't Dahlia. With the right teacher, she could be as good as Dahlia. Someday. He had a lot he could teach her, too.

He also discovered she wasn't as shallow and vain as she appeared. She was a warm, considerate woman and a fantastic person. There was so much more to her than her sex appeal. She listened to him describe just how miserable Connie was to live with and how oppressive she was about with whom he spent his time. Connie was a total square.

Mercedes also liked martinis, but she preferred Cosmos and Appletinis. Flip thought they were a little too sweet for his taste, but the end result was the same. Drinking was a destination. It was a means to blow off steam and set the mood. Drinking made romance more meaningful and fun.

Kevin woke him around ten o'clock Saturday morning with the expectation his father was to take him fishing. "Oh, buddy, I had a really late night. I just don't feel up to it." Nausea from his hangover was brutal.

"But it's not early. It's ten in the morning. You promised, Dad."

"I know, but I just can't do it now. Maybe later. I have a horrible headache this morning."

"Ah, man," Kevin complained. "That's not fair. You said the same thing last week."

"Sorry, little man. But that's life," he mumbled under his pillow. "If you depend on people, they will always disappoint you. It's a lesson you need to learn." And with that pearl of wisdom, he rolled over and went back to sleep.

Mercedes had been soft and comfortable. He loved to be wrapped in her arms. Flip wasn't one of those men who only saw women as sex objects. She was a good listener as well. She truly respected him and seemed inspired by how great his investment strategy was. He even shared with her an idea he had been thinking about to open a Hooter's in Bonners Ferry. He could put it down by the casino where it would draw a lot of business. Canadian men were just like Americans. They all appreciated Hooter's. And their wings were simply awesome. Mercedes was proud when he said if she were a Hooter's girl then she would be a cinch for the calendar. And he meant it, too.

Together, they made Hooter's their next research project and poured a lot of effort into proving a specialized sports bar would be very successful in Bonners Ferry. James Kendall wasn't too sure about the project when Flip finally made the pitch to him.

"Look, Flip," he began. "I'm a Hooter's loving man myself, but that restaurant wouldn't make it in Bonners. You might be able to establish a new business in Bonners, but not one highly specialized like Hooter's.

These local people come from traditional families and wouldn't dream of setting foot in a restaurant like Hooter's."

"Like Hooter's? It's a family-friendly restaurant, sir."

Kendall blinked at him. "Their focus is on sex appeal. In a bigger town, there are enough single men and college kids to keep the place open. In Bonners, most men wouldn't dream of starting a fight with their wives about frequenting such a place."

"Ah, come on. The whole tight shirts and shorts thing is just a gimmick. Their real draw is their food. They have awesome wings."

"Look, Flip. You might be able to open a McDonald's or even an Applebee's in Bonners, but a Hooter's would alienate our very religious community. You would have a fight just to get the business plan through the approval process. The local churches would probably fight you all the way. It's just not going to happen. The answer is no."

Old Man Kendall has lost the edge on his business intuition. There was a day he would have jumped on an all-star idea like this, but the man is just too old and too conservative. Am I the only person left who has a vision for quality of life?

Connie's headaches continued to plague her relentlessly. She was experiencing one migraine a week and sometimes two. For the most part, she was able to work through the pain, but her attention to detail was beginning to diminish. On Wednesday, her till was off by eleven cents and it took her almost an hour to find one simple mistake.

Working so close to Flip was her most significant source of distress. His whole attitude toward her was cold. He hardly spoke to her and he was often heard making fun of "the witch formally known as my wife." He even nicknamed her "She Who Must not be Named."

She'd been told, that someone at work asked him if he knew where she was. He replied, "I don't know, but if you place some candles on the ground in the shape of a pentagram and light them, she will appear."

He had wounded her in so many ways there was little chance of recovery for her, much less for them as a family. She found it increasingly hard to get out of bed and cared nothing about taking a shower and going to work. On many weekends, she didn't even leave her bedroom. If she could stay asleep, then at least her eyes didn't hurt from crying. She began feeding the kids Hot Pockets and frozen pizzas every day rather than cooking for them. She lost a lot of weight and began to look haggard.

She even stopped going to church. The kids still wanted to go, so she would drive them to the church and then pick them up later. Some of the ladies in her Sunday school class reached out to her, but she continually pushed them away. She was simply too embarrassed by Flip's behavior and she couldn't bear to open her door to them. Her assumed shame was destroying her life.

She knew Flip was secretly seeing Mercedes, which drove her mad. She wanted him to get out of their home, but she didn't have the energy to compel him to leave. Being with him in the same room was painful enough at work, but to talk to him at home was excruciating. The pain of knowing he was sleeping with another woman and pretending he wasn't was so intense she simply ignored it. Eventually, he would move out and shack up with his ... friend. Until that time, she would simply suffer and endure the shame she felt.

The kids were experiencing difficulties as well. Ginger was missing her dad, who once took her for walks in the woods behind their house. She missed him getting up with her on the weekends and making waffles or pancakes for everyone to enjoy. That was their special activity together. But Flip was so consumed with his lifestyle he wouldn't take the time to interact with his daughter. She began to avoid him and was just as glad he was too occupied to pay attention to her. Why would she want to be around him anyway when all he did was talk bad about her mother?

Kevin didn't fare much better. His father used to go into the woods with him to shoot arrows or guns or help him build a fort out of fallen trees. Flip used to enjoy fishing with him. Now he spent so much of his time sitting in his workshop with a bottle, he couldn't walk into the woods without risking injury to himself, much less properly handle a gun.

The kids were ever hopeful their father would snap out of his selfishness, but so far he hadn't shown any signs of caring about them in the least. Each time he rejected them, they sank a little deeper into their distrust of him and his motives. The children weren't oblivious to their father's activities. Kevin knew his dad kept a stash of porno magazines out in the workshop and would sneak out there to flip through them while his parents were away.

Ginger spent as much time as possible at her friend Kimee's house. Kimee's family wasn't stable, but at least Kimee would pay attention to her. Sometimes Kimee's stepdad, Randy, would pay attention to her as well. He liked to touch her hair and would even brush it for her when she would let him. She missed her father so much she allowed Randy to cross boundaries with her she knew were inappropriate. It felt good to have a father figure in her life again, even if he was a poor substitute for who her father used to be.

After a few more weeks of his miserable living conditions at home, Flip finally moved out and rented a room at the Kootenai Valley Motel. The rooms were seedy and the clientele were rough, but the rent was cheap. Mercedes wouldn't visit him there, insisting they spend their time together at her house. She told him she wouldn't let him move in with her until more time had passed. She didn't think it would look right for him to move in straight from his wife's house, even though everyone close to them knew what was happening.

While bored at the motel, he spent too much time sipping martinis until he fell asleep watching TV. Drinking was becoming an expensive habit. He was staying up too late drinking and coming to work tired and disheveled. One day, a man in the room next to his offered him a little pick-me-up while they sat in front of their rooms and drank. The pill helped him get his feet under him in the morning and helped him function through the day. Flip knew Old Man Kendall was getting frustrated with him before he started taking the pill and seemed to back off some because his performance improved. At least for the time being. But deep down he knew an addiction to speed was not a good solution to his problem. He was simply creating a worse problem that would manifest itself in the future.

Flip saw his life starting to fall apart. Sometimes he wondered if it could get any worse.

CHAPTER ELEVEN
Justin

"Today is going to be a great day, darling." He was smearing sunscreen on his ears. "And do you know why?"

Connie stepped out of the shower and was drying off. "Because today is the company picnic. Once again I have an opportunity to find out just how wonderful Melanie's kids are. I'll bet that boy of hers fought off an entire regiment of Taliban soldiers all by himself."

He was now rubbing sunscreen on his legs. "If he did, then he deserves our respect. My hat is off to every soldier and sailor in our great country. Even if he can't ski the entire length of Lake Pond Oreille."

"Well, this year, I have something to brag about with my kids."

"Is that right?"

She was slipping into her swimsuit. "I'm going to tell them how Kevin shot a glass bottle with his rifle at five hundred yards. He broke it just like that." She snapped her fingers.

"I should probably clarify the glass bottle was a light bulb, it was in his bedroom, and he was grounded from using his BB gun for six weeks as a result."

Connie shrugged. "If you're only interested in the truth, then you can tell your version. I like mine better. My story makes me happier than your story."

He turned to argue with her but stopped before he could start. "Uh, negative. You will not wear that string bikini to the beach."

She feigned innocence. "But, honey…"

"But nothing. That's not going to happen."

"I thought you liked it."

"Oh, I do like it. It looks wonderful on you. But you aren't getting out of the house with it on. Now take it off."

Connie took a teasingly defensive position. "If you want it off, you have to take it off yourself."

"Is that so?"

"Those are my terms."

"Then it's on!" He charged her and she screamed delightedly. They were going to have a good day.

They endured the burnt hamburgers and smokies and ate watermelon as if it was going out of style until the homemade ice cream made an appearance. And then it was every man for himself. Justin found himself appointed the chief ice cream scooper and began to scoop dollops of ice cream into red Solo cups. The line kept getting shorter until he looked up and there was one person left to be served: Mercedes.

She was dressed in a bikini that would cause Connie's to blush in chagrin. This woman brought new meaning to *va-va-voom*. He had no idea if her tan was real, but she looked like the naughty version of Malibu Barbie.

"Hello, Mr. Grey."

He found her distracting and had trouble not looking at her. "Please, we're at a picnic. You can call me Justin." He filled his scoop with ice cream. "At least today," he said with a smile. "Ice cream?"

"I'm so hot. I really need it. I need you to …" she let the sentence hang in the air on purpose.

Justin had no idea what she was doing. "I beg your pardon? You need me to what?"

She stepped closer. "I need you to smear it all over me." She made the motion of rubbing into her body.

"Uhhh. Well, as diverting as that might be, let's just put it in the little red cup. What do you say?"

"The ball is in your court. You put it where ever you like."

He eyed her warily and handed her the Solo cup. "Enjoy the party."

"You can count on it. I do know how to party."

"Goodbye, now."

"I'll see you around, Justin."

Great. I certainly don't need that kind of attention. As exciting as it may have seemed, he found the situation funnier than flattering. Flattery ended after the first time she flirted with him. Funny began when she couldn't take a hint and made a pathetic attempt to try again. He and Connie would make a good joke of it just as soon as he could find her. And, he realized, he hadn't e-mailed Gerald for a week or so. This would give him a good excuse.

Connie pretended she was jealous, but when she saw how skimpy Mercedes' swimsuit was, she had to laugh with him. For a long moment, she thought the situation funny, and then it became sad. Her heart began to ache for Mercedes because she had so little self-esteem she had to demean herself to gain approval from the men around her at the expense of the approval of her female workmates. When Connie explained what she saw in Mercedes, she thought

Justin felt the conviction too. She knew they both were humbled about poking fun at and laughing about Mercedes.

The situation worsened. Justin ran into Mercedes at the boat ramp. She wandered near him. "Care for a dip?"

"What kind of dip? I like Fritos and bean dip."

Her laugh was clearly manufactured. "No, Justin, care to go deep with me?"

He sighed deeply. "Look, Mercedes, let's put a stop to this. First of all, I'm married to a wonderful woman with whom I have two wonderful children. They mean everything to me and there's nothing I would do to jeopardize that. You'll never know how flattered I am you find me attractive, but you have to understand I can't do it. I can't go there with you. It's just not possible." He shook his head. "I hope you understand me."

"Oh, I understand you just fine, Mr. Grey." As she spoke, her voice grew louder until everyone around them could hear every word she spoke. "And I'll have you know I resent you making me out to be a sex symbol. I tried to be casual with you and you automatically made this out to be about my appearance. And then you speak in code to me about ice cream and how it should be smeared on me. Personally, I find your comments to be inappropriate and I won't stand by and be demeaned by anyone I work for, or with, for that matter." She manufactured tears, "I just want to be left alone. I just want to be happy without the pressure to sleep with my supervisor." And with her last accusation, she wandered down the beach crying into her hands. Several of the women chased after her.

Connie was beside him in a flash. "Well, you did say this was going to be a fun day."

When Gerald received his email about Mercedes and her public accusations, he mentioned he was on his way up and he looked forward to visiting them at Pinehurst. When he arrived at the house, he paused a moment to appreciate the beauty of their home. "I love the stonework in the driveway and how it flows out into paths to the gardens and into the forest. And would you look at this view? Why, you have a full panorama of the mountains in every direction." He paused and enjoyed the moment. "How big is Pinehurst?"

Justin replied, "The house covers over thirty-eight hundred square feet of living space. That doesn't include the three-car garage but does include the unfinished portion of the basement."

"Connie, you have a home to be proud of, and I'm proud for you."

"Thank you," she said graciously. "While we're looking, you might as well see the back yard and the patio." She led them from the driveway along one of the stone paths that once again expanded into a large stonework entertainment area complete with several fire pits. There was a covered pavilion with a water feature draining into what appeared to be a koi pond, at least in the summer. At the end of the pavilion sat an infinity-edge pool that also served as a hot tub on the shallow end. Closer to the house was an extensive three-level wooden deck that began from the back door and extended into the yard connecting the house and the stonework in the patio. Immediately off the backdoor was a small outdoor kitchen that had seen more than one barbecue.

"Why, this is magnificent, Connie. You've built yourself a very nice home."

"Thanks. It helps to have a brother-in-law who is the best general contractor in Northern Idaho."

Gerald winked at her. "You can never go wrong surrounding yourself with quality people. It's hard to soar with eagles when you're surrounded by turkeys, eh?"

Justin laughed casually. "Believe it or not, we still have one thing to do out here. We want to have an ordinary hot tub placed over by the infinity pool. We've found the pool doesn't make as good of a hot tub as we intended. Plus, to make the pool a hot tub, we have to keep the temperature too warm to actually use it for exercise. But that improvement will happen much further down the road." He stopped walking and pointed to the pavilion. "Unless you prefer to talk in my office, we find our patio to be very comfortable."

"It's your home; we play by your rules. Besides, it's an absolutely gorgeous day to be outside." He turned to Connie, "would you join us on the patio? At least for a few minutes?"

"If you like."

He turned to Justin. "How much of this property is yours?"

"We own ten acres here at the house and the back yard joins the national forest."

"Well done." They all sank into the thick-cushioned patio chairs. Gerald reached into the soft leather briefcase he was carrying. "I brought you a gift." He removed a small leather-bound container resembling a very thick personal diary with a key slot. The label read, Glenfiddich, and stamped in silver foil at the bottom of the case, "50-Year Old".

"My goodness," Justin said quietly. "This is too much. I can't take this ..."

"And offend me?" Gerald smiled. "Please, this is a gift."

Justin was humbled. "I don't know what to say. I really wish you hadn't bothered." He accepted the box and saw the flap was locked. He looked to Gerald for clarification.

"Justin, this whiskey is a gift from the Lair. It also comes with this small key. If you notice, it's the same key that opens the cigar lounge at the Westin in Hilton Head. Well, for that matter, every Westin. Congratulations! The men and women of the Lair have extended their hands in the truest sense of friendship and brotherhood and we welcome you to full membership in the Lair, with all the rights and privileges thereof. Your life will never be the same." He turned to Connie, "The reason I wanted you to be here is because you're Justin's wife. He either succeeds or fails based on your support, your wisdom, your intuition, and your keen sense of right and wrong. You're just as much a member of this group as is he. You two are actually one, and we prefer it that way." He paused and very soberly intoned. "Now if you will, bring forth your first-born son, so we can sacrifice him to the gods of the Lair. We shall burn his body in order to sprinkle the ashes into the forest, thereby ensuring new life for generations to come."

Both Connie and Justin stared at him blankly as they tried to process what he just asked of them. Then Gerald broke the tension with a hearty laugh. "Relax, that last part was just for fun. Everyone hears of secret societies and think they have blood initiations, and so forth. We've included that in our induction ceremony for several years now, and it always makes for a good laugh later. Much later, of course. It's actually hard to say without either bumbling it up or laughing. It's such a ridiculous thing." Gerald's light-hearted moment was over and he said, "Do you accept your appointment to the Lair?"

He looked to Connie, who nodded carefully. "We do. We gratefully accept."

Gerald reached into the briefcase again. This time he removed a box holding four, long-stemmed crystal tulip glasses befitting a king.

He handed the box to Connie, who accepted gingerly as if it were a baby.

"Oh, these are beautiful." She opened the box and removed a glass to inspect it closely, holding it carefully by the stem. Each glass bore an inscription that read, "*The Lair*" and showed the date.

Gerald said, "Now if I may? It's tradition to seal your membership with a toast." He handed the key to Justin, who carefully unlocked the case.

"The bottle is hand-blown and finished in Scottish silver by Thomas Fattorini, a sixth-generation silversmith. The bottle alone is a work of art. In the box, you will also find a small leather book and a certificate."

Justin carefully removed the bottle and held it to the light. "Well, this is just magnificent. I don't know what to say."

Connie said, "I do. Thank you, Mr. Alexander."

"Gerald. We're now family. You'll call me Gerald, and you're most welcome, Connie. We're so proud to induct you into our brotherhood. Now, if I may?" He opened the bottle and poured three servings, one for each of them. He lifted his glass and breathed deeply. The pleasure he experienced was akin to a spiritual moment. "The hint of smoke is very subtle."

It was Justin's turn; he'd done this before. "Oak," he announced.

"That's funny," Connie said. "I smell roses."

"Well, now to the fun part." He sipped, allowed the whiskey to sit on his tongue, and then lifted his chin, allowing the Scotch to wash throughout his entire mouth. "Oh, that peat is so subtle. I can hardly taste it."

Justin followed his example and observed, "For me, vanilla and orange."

Connie was not looking forward to actually tasting the scotch as she still compared liquor to cough medicine. She steadied herself and took a small sip. Her senses exploded and she was amazed at what she experienced. "At first it was sweet." She was amazed. "And then I swear I tasted orange."

Gerald smiled warmly. "One does not simply drink a single malt Scotch whiskey. A superb scotch is not something to drink to get drunk or to blow off steam. It is one of the most pleasurable experiences afforded to ordinary man. If done properly, a good scotch will produce a variety of different sensations, all of which should be very positive. Let me demonstrate just how much depth this whiskey has. Connie, would you refill our glasses with about the same measure as before?" He reached into his case and removed a small flask. "Don't worry, this is only Scottish spring water." He added a small amount of water to each glass. "Normally, I abhor anyone altering whiskey with anything, including water or ice. But this is a fifty-year-old Scotch. And one of the finest ever produced, if not the finest. By adding this small amount of pure spring water, the hidden characteristics are revealed. This will probably be the only time you ever see me pour anything into a scotch." He then repeated the tasting process and said, "Can you tell any difference? To me, it's mellower."

Justin said, "I almost taste something that's sweet, like toffee. It's hard to identify."

Connie tasted her sample and closed her eyes. "I don't know what I'm tasting this time, but I feel as though I'm walking through a freshly mown yard just before a rain."

Gerald's eyes beamed. "Connie, you're going to be one of my most favorite members. I look forward to the years ahead of us." He leaned back in his chair and sipped his whiskey with great relish.

After an hour of savoring the gentle mountain air and sharing stories of no great importance, Connie asked, "Gerald, would you stay for dinner?"

He appraised her warmly. "I graciously accept your invitation. Thank you."

When she had gone inside the house, he lit his pipe and said, "Shall we get down to business?" Without waiting for a response, he began. "Your gal, Mercedes, is a dangerous woman. At her last place of employment, she met a man named Rusty Edwards, who was an ambulance-chasing lawyer. He coached her how to set up her boss for a sexual harassment case that netted her the tidy sum of 500,000 dollars. The last time she snared him into sleeping with her at her house, she had a camera that recorded every sordid thing they did and said. The recording included a statement where he promised her a promotion if she would perform a certain act. When they returned to work, Rusty had a copy of the tape delivered to the bank. They threatened to either sue or they would expose the acts and statements. The only way to make them go away was to pay them off. It worked with precision."

"I can only imagine. I'd hate to be at that closed-door meeting."

He chuckled. "You and I both know the bank officers were eating Rolaids for breakfast. Well, Mercedes and Rusty lived high on the hog for a year traveling in Europe and the Caribbean. Before they knew, their money was gone and it was time to try again. For some reason, they picked you as their target. Maybe it was just your year for torment. Maybe God was working this out. Either way, you were the next victim. Only you didn't bite. She has tried several times to snag you, but you always chose properly and never succumbed to her wiles. Righteousness won out if you will. Well, they decided they would simply take the litigation route and accuse you of sexual harassment, hence the scene as the lake. They will try to become such a nuisance the bank will pay them off to go away. It won't be as lucrative, but it will net them enough to move on to the next victim."

"So what do we do now?"

Gerald reached into his bag again and removed two large sealed envelopes. "This has all the evidence you need to destroy them. Give this one to the District Attorney who will see to it they don't prosper anymore. Give this one to your attorney just in case they actually file suit before you can have them arrested. Your attorney will appreciate your help."

"And what do I do to repay you, Gerald?"

His eyes narrowed. "What do you mean?"

"To be honest, I don't want to jump from the frying pan into the fire. I don't want to use this information if it's going to cost me something from you down the line. I'd simply be trading silver shackles for golden shackles. But I would still be in bondage."

Gerald exhaled slowly. "Justin, I don't think you understand how this works. There is very little you can offer me. I'm sponsoring *you*. That means I am responsible for you and for your well-being. I'm investing everything I have in you and your family. You'll take my place someday and we want you to be the right person. Which means I'm now your, say, godfather.

Justin smiled to himself as he recalled he'd once tagged Gerald as the Godfather.

"You and I are in a covenant with each other. What I have is yours. What you have is mine …" He held up a gentle hand to assuage Justin's concerns. "Relax, you have nothing I want or need, save your friendship. Justin, what I … what we … are giving you is bigger than the lottery. It's bigger than all the lotteries. You're now connected with the largest economic power in the world. This is why we tested you at the conference. We had to know if you were trustworthy. Your bond of commitment to your wife is one of the most important relationships you'll ever have. If you aren't faithful to her, then you won't be faithful to anything else. That's why we tested you. And we're proud you came through with flying colors."

"Well, not so much, Gerald." The topic was still a little hot for him. "You placed me in a dangerous situation. What if I had compromised? You could have destroyed me in ways I can't even imagine. You could have destroyed my family—our lives."

"Yes, I know." He was matter of fact. "*To whom much is given, from him much will be required.* Please forgive me, but I had to know you were trustworthy. My wife died over a year ago. My son is serving two life sentences for murdering a cop. I have no legacy to leave except through you. You're worthy of what I'm about to give you.

"You'll now be advising the President of the United States on matters great and small. You will be consulting with heads of states in places you have never even heard of, and you'll be consulting in all matters of earthly importance to people beyond your ability to imagine. We simply had to know, Justin. It's that big. There's that much at stake."

He had no idea how to respond, so he simply held his tongue.

Gerald reached into his case one last time and removed a leather-bound folder. "This is my net worth. It's now yours, as well."

Justin opened the folder and almost fell out of his chair. "Oh, my!"

"Rather astounding, eh?"

"You have more wealth than Bill Gates ever had."

"There are many of us in that category. There is an entire society of us and the world doesn't even know it. We thrive on secrecy, and we do thrive. Justin, I have selected you to be my heir. Please forgive me for hiring the prettiest prostitute in all of history to tempt you. I had to know."

Justin closed his eyes for a moment. "You have no idea just how close I came to falling."

Gerald exhaled slowly. "She had to be tempting. If there was no temptation, then there was no threat." He sat quietly and allowed Justin to process the enormity of what had been laid upon him. When he was satisfied Justin had adapted, he moved on to the next phase. "I have made some funds available to you for your immediate use. It's been my experience when someone falls into advanced wealth they often lose that wealth rather quickly, and they're worse off than they were before. So, I'm allocating fifteen million for you to use for random things, such as upgrading your church facilities, or adding a new library to your school, or for local charity work. Use the money as a slush fund until you're accustomed to handling this kind of wealth. If you spend it all, then there is no real harm done. Consider the money your petty cash fund.

"I'm also allocating one hundred million for you to use as an investment. I have been following your work on the restaurant investments James Kendall shot down. Personally, I liked the idea. But I'm wondering if you shouldn't go larger?"

"Larger? How?"

"Well, that's up to you. Let's make it your trial run to see just how intuitive you really are. Think big. You want to try and capture the people who are already coming through Bonners Ferry. See if you can find a way to draw an even larger crowd. Generate your own crowd. If we lose this money, well—it's only money. But I have a feeling you'll succeed."

"Has this ever been tried before?"

Gerald laughed. "In fact it has. Remember Norm from the convention? He's from North Dakota. When we invested in him, he managed to transform the entire state by tapping into the oil and gas industry. The North Dakota economy is the fastest growing economy in the Western Hemisphere. If the government left us alone, we could single-handedly reverse this stupid recession, but don't get me started. I get political really fast when it comes to government interference. No more of that. I can see from your wife's expression she is ready for us to come in and eat. God bless her, I hope she made the lasagna she made so famous."

CHAPTER TWELVE
Flip

Mercedes finally got what she wanted from Flip one night while engaging with him in her bedroom. At a heightened moment, she began to tease him, luring him into her trap. She finally found the thing that inspired him the most and said, "You know what would make this moment even better? If you promised me a promotion at work, I would make this a daily habit." Before Flip knew what happened, he had given her the keys to the kingdom and said everything she wanted him to say.

Rusty Edwards delivered the bad news to Flip the next morning as he was shaving in front of the mirror at the motel. At first he was sick to his stomach, and then stark terror filled his heart as realization flooded over him.

James Kendall was less than enthusiastic as Flip explained to him what happened, and how he placed them all in a bad situation. "You'll pay for this, Flip. I promise you."

"Sir, I had no idea this was going to happen."

"Of course you didn't, you twit," he roared. "I certainly hope you wouldn't have bedded her if you'd known this was going to happen, although I'm starting to wonder just how selfish you can be. You have

... er, you had a really good thing at home. You had a wonderful wife and amazing kids, and a good future. But not anymore. All of that is now gone and was finalized this morning. The bank will end up paying for your stupidity and that makes me want to pop your little head right off of your shoulders." He stood from his desk and began to pace back and forth. "How dare you? How could you be so stupid to allow that woman to flash you some skin and then you give away the farm? Especially when you had such a good thing at home?"

"So," Flip asked gingerly. "What are we going to do about it?"

"We?" Kendall roared. "Surely you understand you no longer work here? Or do I have to draw you a picture? The bank will have to pay through the nose for your entertainment. She will prove to be the most expensive prostitute you've ever enjoyed, and she was paid for by someone else." He shook his head and sat back down. "What I would do for a cup of coffee," he said regretfully. "Please collect your things and be out of the office by the end of the day. Now if you will leave? I have to contact my legal team."

Connie thought she'd suffered as much shame as possible until Kendall called her into his office and broke the news to her. Up to this point, she was going to lose her marriage; now she was going to lose her home and financial security as well. How much more could she take? Would there ever be an end to this downward spiral? One useful thing Kendall did for her before giving her the rest of the day off was give her some legal advice. "I recommend you consult an attorney. There may be a chance you can salvage your retirement funds and some of your assets before they're consumed by whatever lawsuit is about to fall upon you."

She took his advice to heart and found an attorney who was skilled in family law. Based on his legal opinion, she initiated a lawsuit for divorce. Maybe she could beat Mercedes to the punch.

Ginger was spending most of her free time at Kimee's home to avoid the pain she experienced at the hands of her own parents. Her mother was so lethargic at home she might as well not exist. And as far as Ginger cared, her father no longer existed. She would occasionally call him on his cell phone, but he never initiated contact with her. And the few times she was able to talk to him, he seemed to be in a hurry to do something else. He didn't have time for her.

Kimee's dad, Randy, kept telling Ginger she was a girl of rare beauty and that she had all the makings of being the next top model. He told her about a friend of his who was a talent agent and who was looking for some new faces to sell to a magazine he worked for in Denver. He arranged for her to bring some swimsuits and several changes of clothes and then spent the better part of a weekend taking photos of the girls for his friend. The photos were fairly innocent, with the girls posing in fun, teenage shots that were full of smiles and happiness. He even told the girls if his friend bought the photos, they would have as much as five hundred dollars to spend however they wanted.

The next time Ginger saw Randy, he told her his friend loved the photos and was interested in buying them, but he wanted some different poses. He wanted to see the girls dressed in towels and hidden behind things like balloons or feathers. Without a second thought, the girls participated in the photos, already thinking of some clothes at the mall they wanted, not to mention the new Hollister hoodie that was all the rage.

Soon, Randy announced his friend was ready to buy and had even sent fifty dollars to the girls as a down payment. He wanted them to take more photos, but this time with no towels. He didn't take any photos that were too revealing, but he posed them lying on their stomachs just like the other models and teenage stars they saw in magazines.

Randy then announced his friend wanted the photos and was willing to pay top dollar for them. But this time he wanted action shots that were wildly and illegally inappropriate, but very exciting. Randy was to be the male model in the photos. That day Ginger lost her innocence and changed her life forever.

Randy proceeded to tell her his actions were her fault and she would get in trouble if she told anyone what had happened. If her mother found out, she would probably lose her job, and her father might even go to jail. But, if she returned for more visits, he would keep what happened a secret and no one would ever know what a bad girl she really was.

The whole matter was very confusing to her. She knew what Randy wanted her to do was wrong, but he was able to awaken feelings in her she had no idea existed. Despite how wrong she felt while doing those things, they were strangely exciting too. She knew what happened had to be kept a secret and she deeply feared someone was going to find out. Most of all, she didn't want her mom to lose her job because of something she had done.

As the weeks progressed, she grew a bit less uncomfortable with her activities at Kimee's house. Randy kept telling her to relax so things would go quickly, but she was still struggling with the whole matter. Finally, he decided she needed some little pills to make her relax. Before long, she looked forward to taking the pills, and even kept a few for herself to use when she was at home.

Kevin fared no better. The more his father pushed him away, the angrier he became. For many months, he refused to blame his mother for anything that happened. But as the anger stirred within him, the more he focused his rage against her for not doing anything to stop what was happening. Both of his parents were failing him and his sister had left him to rot in his house all by himself.

He spent much of his time devouring the magazines his father left behind, which kindled a smoldering fire in him that demanded more fuel with each passing month. He found a new friend at school named Chet, who not only had magazines Kevin had never heard of but also had movies.

Chet was into martial arts and spent a lot of time teaching Kevin the forms, punches, and kicks he learned in Taekwondo. They spent many hours at Chet's house sparring in the backyard. Kevin was finding a way to channel his anger and his fighting skill was growing.

One day at school, a new kid smarted off to him in an attempt to become the new tough kid on the block. Kevin snapped. When Kevin tapped into his anger, his rage surfaced. The fight lasted no more than twenty seconds. With a flash of short punches and knee thrusts, the boy was sent to the ER with a missing tooth and needing stitches on his lips. Kevin went home with a three-day suspension, but, instead of feeling contrition for his actions, he felt purged and excited. Now he had a means of channeling his negative emotions and hatred. For the first time in months, he felt good.

CHAPTER THIRTEEN
Justin

Justin spent many weeks contemplating how to draw new travelers to Bonners Ferry. He already knew the steady flow of Canadians created a large pool of visitors, but to draw new people who had no intention of going to North Idaho was an entirely different proposition. North Idaho wasn't exactly close to the bulk of the population in the Western United States. Bonners Ferry was a place people drove through, not to. So, why should they drive here specifically?

His family was enjoying his new freedom to become an entrepreneur. Justin formed a new company, Grey Matters, Inc., and busied himself with the details of launching the new enterprise. His first official act as CEO of Grey Matters was to hire a new personal secretary. He knew immediately who would be the first person to interview.

Janet and Mercedes had once competed against each other for his secretarial position at the bank and he'd allowed Mercedes' ski bunny look to influence him. Janet was his best applicant, but beauty often moved business transactions faster than competence, so he chose poorly. When Janet didn't gain employment at the bank, she accepted a secretarial office job at a landscaping company in Sandpoint. Essentially, she answered phones and filed papers. The job didn't pay well, but she had to work somewhere. When he contacted her about a personal secretary position, she was excited.

"Could you tell me more about the work, sir?"

"I will need a personal secretary to work with me in managing the various investments and research conducted by Grey Matters. We're just getting started, but as the need surfaces, I will hire an office assistant to help you with the tedious day to day tasks you won't have time to manage."

Her freckled cheeks and nose gave her a special charm, but her smile set her apart from other women. "So, you don't want me to clean bathrooms and file?"

He appreciated her point. "You will be my personal assistant. We can hire a college kid to perform tasks like that. What do you say?"

Another matter he needed to resolve was his involvement at the bank. Justin explained to Kendall he was moving in a new direction. "Sir, I have a private investor who wants me to focus strictly on his projects. I will work exclusively for him. Of course, I will stay until you find a suitable replacement."

Kendall wouldn't hear of it. "I don't know what you're talking about, Justin. You belong at this institution." He sipped his tea and smiled. "I finally found a blend I like. But I had to go all the way to Seattle to find it. Have you ever visited the Teavana store? Anyway, they have a Peach Bellini something or the other that's pretty nice. Would you care for a cup?"

He didn't want a cup of tea, as he preferred coffee, but if Mr. Kendall was excited about the tea, he wanted to support him. "Thank you, that would be nice."

Kendall busied himself preparing a second tea set. Justin found it absurd and amusing Kendall could be so enthusiastic about something so … un-Marine, for lack of a better description. "The tea has to steep for seven minutes. But don't worry, my pot has already steeped and is ready to go. And look at this!" He held up a sugar bowl with small rocks in it. "These are sugar crystals. They almost taste like molasses. Go on, try one."

Justin complied and almost laughed watching Kendall sit practically on the edge of his seat with excitement. "Yes, there is a very faint molasses edge." For a moment, he mentally tried to compare the sugar to the scotch, but the analogy fell apart before it came together.

Kendall shoved a cup of tea in front of him and motioned for him to add the sugar crystals. He lifted the cup and saw the Marine Corps emblem of the eagle, globe, and anchor decorated it. Kendall might have been forced away from his coffee, but he was still a Devil Dog at heart.

Justin dutifully sipped the tea. "It's not bad," he managed, which was high praise for him.

Kendall nodded and said, "Now what's this business about you leaving us?"

"I'm going in another direction. I have a private investor who wants me to work exclusively for him. I simply won't have time for both jobs."

"Well, you can't leave the bank. I won't hear of it."

"Sir, I don't see any other way. My working at two places wouldn't be fair to the bank, and I've already agreed to work with my investor."

Kendall eyed him knowingly. "Does this investor have anything to do with the Lair?"

Justin smiled. "He does."

Kendall crinkled his forehead in thought. "Well, we can't let that opportunity pass, can we? So, you leave me no choice. Justin, you're fired."

"What? Fired?"

Kendall laughed. "Only for the effect. I accept your resignation, but I insist you become a member of the board."

"I probably won't have time to participate in many board meetings."

"Balderdash! That doesn't matter. I'm not going to have a member of the Lair get away from me without riding his coat tails for a little ways."

"Mr. Kendall, I've never said I was a member of the Lair."

"Yes, yes. So noted. But we will still need your name attached to this institution in some way. And, please, call me Kendall. After all, we're friends."

In the big picture, Justin had other plans as well; plans that involved his family. He'd seldom set aside time in the year to take his family on special vacations. He always considered his work too consuming to step away for more than a few days at a time.

When Gerald visited them at his house, he'd said, "When we were at the convention, do you remember how I said there were a few issues in your life that make you vulnerable?"

"Uh, oh, here we go again," he said with a smile.

"Are you ready for the next issue I would like to address?"

He exhaled slowly. "Yes, let's be done with it. I'm ready."

"Justin, this might seem trivial, but it's not. It's as big as your sexual indiscretions. You have a tendency to spend more time at work than you do at home. You only have so many years to invest in your children's lives. And trust me that, from my personal perspective, is a mistake you don't want to make. How important are your children? Are they more valuable to you than your work? This is a tricky problem because God created men to find great meaning and satisfaction in their work. So many men make work their identity. And it starts so small. You're young and you get married right out of college. You start a career and a family about the same time. To have a successful career, you have to invest a large amount of time into it from the very beginning. Even after you've successfully established your career, you can't find a way to back off because you're too involved.

"With most men, it's either work or family. We've always struggled to create balance in this area. But what is more important? Children or career? You can work a career your entire lifetime if you so choose, but you only have your children in your home for about twenty years. So, I always ask, which one of your choices is eternal? And I always ask—which one do you want to surround you on your deathbed? Your best clients or your children?

"I firmly believe that most of the problems in our society are a result of fathers not spending enough time with their children. We don't take the time to lead them, and guide them, and show them how to be good fathers and husbands. Our children grow up fatherless when their father is right there. What a tragedy! It's too bad our society values our economy so much that our children are sacrificed.

"Well, I guess I've preached enough, and I think I've made my point." He made sure Justin was looking at him. "Your kids are the only legacy that will matter. The rest is all vanity."

Of course, Gerald was right. Justin was guilty as charged. He couldn't change the past, but he could look to the future. That October, he arranged for them to take one month and focus only on themselves. He found a Mediterranean cruise that left out of Barcelona and toured France, Italy, Greece, and Turkey. They could make the effort to visit each of those countries individually, or arrange for those countries to come to them, which is the benefit of a cruise. You go to bed in France, and you wake up in Italy.

"Now that's the way to vacation," he said with a smile.

Connie was excited. She'd always said a Mediterranean cruise was a dream of hers. "And how long is it?"

"Twelve days."

"Oh, how wonderful! What do you say, kids?"

Kevin shrugged and said, "Please pass the mashed potatoes," and then burst out into laughter. "That sounds awesome!"

Ginger was excited as well, but her smile faded quickly. When prompted, she replied, "last week you asked us what we'd rather do. You gave us the choice between Disney World and a cruise."

"That was a hard decision," Connie agreed. "But we're going to Europe! I'm very excited about that. Aren't you, Ginger?"

Ginger thought about it. "Yeah, I'm excited. But when we voted, Kevin and I voted for Disney."

Justin held up his hand. "Patience, Grasshopper."

"Huh?"

"Sorry. You aren't old enough to appreciate that reference. But, you're old enough to appreciate this—when we get back from Europe, we will go to Disney World for ten days."

The room erupted in screams of elation. Had someone been walking past, they would have assumed the children were being slaughtered in the dining room. They broke into a chorus of "Thank you, Dads," that went on for several seconds.

"I have a plan; see if this works for everyone. We will fly to London for a day or two, and then we will take the train to Paris for a day or two. Next we go to Barcelona and board the cruise ship for twelve days. When we dock in Istanbul, we will fly to Orlando and spend the next ten days at Disney. I don't know if there is enough to do to take up ten days. The Disney woman I talked to assured me we would have a magical trip and at the end of ten days would still want one more."

"Cool," Kevin observed.

"The Disney woman also told me that they're having a special thing called, 'Mickey's Not So Scary Halloween Party.' You can dress up in a Halloween costume and trick or treat right there in the park. How does that sound?"

"Totally wicked!" Ginger announced.

"Where will we stay?" Connie was always a practical woman.

"The room I booked is in a Disney resort called the Yacht Club. The woman said they have some awesome resorts to stay at, but this one is walking distance from EPCOT and from Hollywood Studios. She said we can't go wrong with this plan."

Connie looked at Kevin. "Go get my computer. We need to check this out. And we need to start right now."

Justin and Janet began pouring over ideas of how to draw a crowd to Bonners Ferry but kept coming up short. Janet had grown up in California and was fairly new to the area. "The reason we moved here was because we wanted a fresh start after my husband died. All of our memories were so connected with our home we couldn't move on past his death."

"I'm so sorry," Justin said. "How did he die?"

Janet shook her head. "He had a weird accident. He was coming down the stairs, tripped, and broke his neck on the way down. My daughter found him when she got home from school. Horrible!"

"Oh, no!" he lamented. "So you left California?"

"We tried living there for a while, but we couldn't handle all the memories. We sold our home and moved. I found a job in Spokane as a research analyst, but the company went bankrupt just weeks after I took the job. We were already moved to the area and we loved the beautiful national forests and the mountains, so we decided to stay. The economy's hard here, but I finally found that job at the landscaping company. I'm so glad you called. We were sinking fast. The timing couldn't have been better.

"Anyway, one thing I've noticed about Bonners Ferry is there are no family-oriented activities here unless you're into the whole forest thing. That's great, but you can't be in the forest all the time. And in the winter, there are some great skiing and snowmobiling activities, but you can't do that all the time, either. So, this idea came to me last weekend. We went to Silverwood Theme Park in Coeur d'Alene, which was fun and all. We enjoyed the roller coasters and what not, but when we decided to go to the water park, we almost froze our tails off in the middle of summer—the water was so cold.

"When was this? Last week, did you say?"

"Yep. Here we are in summer, but the temperature is in the upper seventies. It's wonderful, but a tad cool for swimming."

"And?" he prompted.

"And I was thinking—what we need is a large, indoor water park."

His brow furrowed, "I don't know. There are water parks in Coeur d'Alene already."

"But, they're only open for a few months."

"Not Triple Play. It's indoor."

"I'm talking about the biggest and best indoor water park, one that makes Triple Play look like a hotel swimming pool."

"Still, I don't know."

"Follow me on this, Justin. This should be a multifaceted park. I want to have everything you could possibly want. There should be a water park, but there should also be an indoor jogging track around the perimeter. That's one drawback of the Inland Northwest—the rain and the snow. The snow season lasts for around five months, depending on the year. That's five months that health conscious people can't run. And they certainly can't swim."

"Okay, I get that part. But that's not enough."

"I agree. That's why we're going to put in a Bass Pro Shop. But this one is going to connect to the indoor park—we'll have a place where people can fish from an indoor stocked stream. We will have an indoor rifle and archery range. Think about it, we can draw the families into town with the water park. If dad doesn't want to float in the lazy river with his wife, he can rent a pole and go drown worms in our fishing area. Or he can rent a rifle and get in some target practice."

"Are you sure you're from California?"

She was on a roll and ignored him. "Can you imagine how many local businesses would want to host a convention in the offseason when they could offer that kind of entertainment for their clients?"

"And where will these people stay?"

"Hello? They will have to stay in the really nice Hilton we're going to build, complete with meeting rooms and everything else."

"And if we added a steak house…"

"It would be a compliment to the Baskin-Robbins you want to build."

"Which would go great in the middle of a water park," he was catching the vision. "But you're missing something."

"Oh?"

"We need a driving range. Golf is a big sport for people suffering from the winter blues."

And just like that Eagle Summit Resort was launched. They bought all the land surrounding the Three Mile intersection and broke ground on the world's largest indoor water park and resort, even surpassing the Ocean Dome in Miyazaki, Japan. The entire complex was massive, covering more than 350,000 square feet, which included the driving range and the indoor fishing park.

Before the complex broke ground, Grey Matters built a Famous Dave's Barbeque and a McDonalds, all of which brought great trepidation to Kendall, who insisted that Justin had fallen off the turnip truck.

When word got out that Eagle Summit Resort was financially solvent, new investors began to look into the opportunities surrounding Bonners Ferry. Restaurants and hotels began sniffing around, trying to determine if there was room for them to jump in and test the water.

CHAPTER FOURTEEN
Flip

Connie's divorce had been final for a year—the only anniversary she cared to observe anymore. Their properties were finally settled, but she didn't net much from the settlement. She wanted to keep Pinehurst, but their home was too expensive for her to maintain on a teller's salary. On perhaps the saddest day of their lives, Connie and the kids moved from their home in Pleasant Valley on the edge of Bonners Ferry to a small rental she found next to the Safeway grocery store. At least she didn't have to go far to buy groceries.

She likened the experience of losing Pinehurst to having her closest family member die from a disease that took years. On her last day at Pinehurst, she stepped from the front door for the last time, held the kids in a tight hug, and wept openly. She had intended for her grandchildren to spend their summers playing in the forest behind the house and swimming in her small pool. Justin had plans to build a fairy playground complex near the greenhouse, one of those wooden playgrounds with a castle and a climbing wall where the slide spirals down from the very top of the tower.

She absolutely hated to lose her garden, as working with plants and the soil was one of her favorite pastimes. "Such a waste," she muttered.

She and the kids walked through the garden gate and toured the raspberry plants and the apple trees one last time. She almost collapsed when they strolled past the tree house Justin built for Ginger when she was five. They were losing more than a house. They were losing their identities and their future. They were losing the family reunions around the patio, the weekend slumber parties, and the backyard campouts. Ginger cried inconsolably when they paused and whispered goodbye to Gracie, the Beagle that helped raise the kids. She was buried under a large weeping willow in the corner of the garden.

All they were and all they would ever be was represented by this magnificent house. And they were practically giving it away because neither party could afford to keep it. Kevin spent a few moments searching under the willow tree for the pocketknife he lost when he turned ten, just days after receiving it for his birthday. He was certain the knife fell out of his pocket as he climbed the tree, but he had never known for sure what happened to it.

Connie always planned for Ginger to be married under the arch that marked the path from the garden to the patio. August was such a pretty month for weddings in North Idaho. The rainy summer was usually over by then and the fall weather was just promising to bring slightly cooler mornings and evenings. She always said, "If you live in Bonners Ferry, have an outdoor wedding in August—perhaps the prettiest month of the year."

Their new home was small but comfortable—a good, clean rental. Her biggest problem was she didn't want to live there, considering she had one of the nicest homes in Bonners Ferry—or at least used to have one of the nicest homes.

Even with their reduced monthly bills, Connie was not able to survive on her teller income. She had to find a second job. After weeks of placing resumes all over town, she finally found an opening for part a part-time bookkeeper at Davis Farm Implements. Her new boss, Ben Simpson, was married to a friend of hers who used to work at the bank years ago. Sandy quit one day and was never heard from again. Everyone thought she went to Seattle to live with her mother.

Ben was a dark and moody man who didn't smile and was seldom seen in a good mood. Most people described him as unapproachable but otherwise harmless. What did it matter to her? She was only keeping the books and that was a job she could accomplish in only a few hours on a weekend. She had little interaction with Ben.

Ginger withdrew from their lives as much as possible. She was sullen and moody and spent most of her time locked in her bedroom with the music blaring. Connie tried to be patient with her, but Ginger didn't make it easy. She was hostile towards both her parents, but Connie caught most of the flak because she was the only parent who actually had a presence in her life.

Ginger had become careless about her grooming and was disinterested in bathing. Her sleeping patterns varied radically as she spent most nights awake and slept as much during the day as possible. Connie missed all the symptoms that Ginger was using drugs even though her eyes were red and glassy. Connie reasoned that Ginger would go through spurts where she had plenty of energy and seemed happy followed by periods when she would be miserable. Ginger had never been overweight, but now she was very skinny, even gaunt. Only when small items began to disappear did Connie start to wonder what was happening.

One Wednesday, Connie came home during her lunch break and searched Ginger's room. At the bottom of the clothes hamper, she found small strips of foil and some plastic baggies with a substance that resembled brown sugar.

Terror seized her. Connie had found meth in her daughter's room. A horror that she had never known existed overwhelmed her and her hands started shaking.

Ginger, of course, denied that she had a problem. Before she denied having a problem, she denied even knowing what meth was and went so far to accuse her brother of hiding the drugs in her clothes hamper. But, when Connie pressed her for the truth, Ginger broke down and came clean amidst many tears of remorse.

"Do you want help, honey? Do you care?"

Ginger nodded a tearful and snotty yes.

"Come on, baby. Let's do this. I have no idea what to do, so let's go to the ER and get started."

The next day, Connie consulted with the social worker at the hospital. She had so many questions about drug rehab she didn't know where to start. The first big question would determine how the rest were managed. "So, who pays for drug rehab?"

Reba looked at her over her glasses and said, "That's the big question, isn't it? Well, the answer depends on several different factors. Your insurance will cover some of it, but not all. There are grants available, but your income has to meet a certain threshold, and I'm afraid you made too much last year."

Connie was cold inside. "But we're barely making ends meet. Last year I had to file jointly with my husband, but now we're divorced."

Reba frowned. "I know. And I know how horrible that is, but the grants have very strict guidelines. There are some state programs that might be able to help, but then you won't have the luxury of private rehab."

Connie pulled at a loose string on her sleeve. "Luxury isn't a word we often use at our house." A tear formed in her eye. "I guess we have no choice." She fidgeted in her chair. "Where is the state facility?"

"Boise."

Connie was incredulous. "Boise? That's an eight-hour drive from here."

Reba was sympathetic. "I know, Connie. I know how horrible your situation is. I wish there were another way."

She stared at the ceiling for a moment. "I barely have enough gas to run around town, much less drive to Boise and back. I wish there were some church that could help, or some donor."

Reba sighed deeply. "There are churches that will help, but there aren't any church-sponsored rehab centers close. I think the nearest one is in California." She looked at her paperwork. "It says here that you attend Bonners Ferry Community Church. I imagine they can help you with gas money if you ask."

Shame. Shame caused her to close her eyes in defeat. "I haven't attended in a long time—since well before the divorce. I just couldn't face them after all that Flip put us through."

"What about the kids? Do they go to a youth group anywhere?"

"At Bonners Ferry Community Church." She opened her eyes with some effort. "But they don't go very often anymore." Her lips pressed together and her eyes narrowed. "I've failed them. I was so caught up in my own problems that I failed my children." A deep ache in her chest caused her to groan. "But I will do better. I will get her the help she needs."

"That's a good start, Connie. You can probably meet with Pastor Sukcow today if you give him a call."

"Who?"

"Bill Sukcow. He's the new pastor at Bonner Community."

"But what happened to … Pastor Davis?"

"He retired a little over a year ago."

Connie was sad. She'd loved Pastor Davis and regretted how she kept pushing him away when he tried to meet with her during the early days of her separation. That afternoon she met with Bill Sukcow and explained her situation to him. He was a young man with a hard jaw line and hair that was prematurely graying. As soon as she saw him, she compared him to a televangelist she used to watch on TV when she was young. Bill listened with concern until she finished explaining what was wrong.

"And you're a member here?"

Connie hesitated. "Yes, I am. My husband and I used to attend here before we divorced."

"And when was that?"

"What, the divorce or the attendance?"

"Both, actually."

She sighed. "We divorced last year. Actually, it was over a year ago. We stopped coming the year before that."

"So where do you attend now?"

Connie cringed. What was that tone in his voice? "We don't. I don't."

"Well, Connie, why not? Our darkest times are when we should seek God, not when things are happy."

The ache was building in her chest again. "Pastor, I know what you're saying. We … I … am going through a hard time. I'm trying to get my feet under me, but I have a hard time doing it."

Bill turned to his computer and tapped a few keys. "I see you've been lifelong members of this church. Looks like your husband taught the couple's class for a long time."

"My ex-husband."

"I know this is a personal question, but you've come to me for help. I need more information. Why did you divorce?"

Did she really have to go through this again? "My husband cheated on me while on a business trip."

"I'm so sorry to hear that. Was it just that one time?"

"While we were a couple, yes."

"And did you seek counseling from anyone?"

"No." She could tell he was going to ask the follow-up question, so she beat him to it. "Flip wouldn't go."

"Flip?" He looked at his computer screen. "I have Justin as your husband."

"My ex-husband. His name is Justin, but he decided to go by Flip in the last few years. He wanted to reinvent himself."

"Okay, so Flip refused to attend counseling. What about you?"

Here we go. This is where he points out how weak I was. She shook her head in frustration. What was done could not be reversed no matter how wrong she was. "I wanted to, but …" She lost the energy to finish.

"But what, Connie?" Bill seemed more like a frustrated high school football coach than a pastor. "Everyone has a "but." Some buts are bigger than others. Your butt needs to be brought to church."

Connie felt trapped. Had he rehearsed that little spiel? "Pastor, I know I've made mistakes. I've lost everything I have since my … ex-husband went to a convention and bagged a whore. The only thing I have that survived the last year was my children. And now Ginger …" the tears were threatening again. How much grieving did she have to endure? "And now my Ginger is lost as well." She tried to stop the tears, but to no avail. What she needed now was a tissue. She dug through her purse but couldn't find one. "I'm sorry, Pastor …"

"What exactly are you sorry for, Connie?"

"Because I need a tissue and I don't have any."

"Oh," he said blankly. He reached across his desk and pulled a tissue for her.

"Thank you. Could I have more than one?"

He grabbed the box and set it in front of her. "Connie, I want to help you. I really do. But the recession has hit us pretty hard, too. We have the expansion project going on that's taking all of our extra funds. And I've been burned before by people who claim to be part of my church, who say they're with me no matter what. But in the end, they just wanted something from me. So, here's what I need from you, Connie. I need a commitment from you. I need to see you sitting in one of those pews on Sunday. You've got to get back into church. You need us. We need you. What do you say?"

"I will be in Boise on Sunday because that is where my daughter will attend rehab. I can't be here on Sunday."

"We need some kind of commitment here, Connie. At least set up some counseling sessions for next week. My calendar is open. I don't have many counseling sessions set up at all."

Connie's strength was failing her. "Pastor, what I need right now is the money to take my daughter to rehab and back." What she wanted to say was, *we can figure out the rest later, can't we*? But what she said was, "Never mind. I'll find the money somewhere." And she got up to leave.

Bill stood up as well. "Connie, we want to help you. Why don't you sit down and we will work this out?"

She slowly shook her head. Her heart had bled enough for one day. *Lord, how I miss Pastor Davis. He was such a good man and a caring man.* She stepped through the open door to the receptionist's office and came face to face with Betty, the church secretary for the last twenty years or so. Betty's face immediately melted when she saw Connie's distress.

"Connie?" Bill's voice came from behind her. "Come back in and sit down. Please?"

She sadly turned her back and pressed by Betty. She needed some fresh air. She also felt as though she was going to throw up. *Please let me make it to the flower bed outside the door.* She barely made it outside before losing what was left of her sandwich.

She heard heels clicking on the sidewalk behind her. "Oh, Connie," Betty bent over her. "Come back inside."

"Can't," she said as she retched again.

"Enough of that. Let's get you inside to the bathroom where we can wash your face." Betty wasn't asking; she lifted Connie by the arms and almost carried her into the bathroom down the hall. Betty washed her face and brushed her hair out of her face. "Come on, let's go to the Flower Garden. You need to sit for a minute."

The Flower Garden was a Sunday school room for the Adult Three group. The old ladies in the class were tired of the décor in the room and decided turning the room into a flower patch would be lovely. The room was beautiful, but anyone with allergies needed to steer clear. The carefully cultivated arrangements made for a peaceful setting and some carefully placed couches in the corner made the room comfortable.

Betty sat Connie carefully on the corner couch and whispered, "How about a cup of tea?"

"That would be nice. Thank you." *What is happening to me? How did my life come to this?* She wanted to get up and leave, but she didn't have the strength. The couch was comfortable and the room smelled pretty. In a flash, Betty was back with tea and a small plate of cookies.

"Thank you, Betty. You shouldn't trouble yourself."

"Don't you fret about that, Connie. I'm so sorry about what's happened to you. You've been on our prayer list for quite a while, you know?"

"Thank you."

Betty pushed the plate closer to her. "Take a Nutter Butter. They're my favorites."

Connie smiled. "Mine, too." After a cup of tea and a few cookies, she was feeling much better.

Betty sat with her and quietly caught her up to speed about which church members had died in the past year and who was now homebound. She poured herself a new cup of tea and said, "Connie, I'm so sorry about Bill Sukcow. What he did and said was inappropriate. He's our interim pastor. The search committee is still looking for a replacement for Pastor Davis. Those are some hard shoes to fill."

Connie had no reply. She felt bad enough for not knowing that Pastor Davis had retired.

Betty placed her cup on her saucer. "Bill is a terrible pastor. He's very young and he has very little experience. He just doesn't have the knack for the job. So, please, excuse him. He's just in over his head, that's all." She smiled apologetically.

Connie could tell Betty was concerned about her. She knew her hair was flat and almost stringy, her face gaunt, and her eyes hollow. She'd been through the very fires of Hell lately. The old, witty Connie appeared to be gone forever.

"What can we do to help you?" Betty gently asked.

Connie almost bolted. "Nothing. I will manage on my own."

"No, Connie, I won't stand for it. We're a family and we will take care of you. Now tell me what you need. I'll talk to the finance committee and get you help."

Connie spent a few minutes outlining what she needed to transport Ginger to Boise in the morning. Betty made a few mental notes and promised to get in touch with her by the end of the day.

That evening, Connie met Betty on her front porch and accepted a small envelope from the church.

Betty quickly returned to her car. "Jim's waiting for supper, don't you know."

In the envelope, Connie found a Hallmark card and five hundred dollars cash—enough money to get her to Boise and back, and then to make the return trip thirty days later. *Thank you, Lord*, she muttered under her breath. *The church has been good to me, but I'm not going back until Pastor Bill is replaced.*

Saturday morning was cold and rainy as she and Ginger drove from Bonners Ferry on their southward journey to Boise.

This is going to be a long weekend.

CHAPTER FIFTEEN
Justin

Justin was an automatic nominee to chair the search committee to find a replacement for Pastor Davis, a man who meant more to them and to the community than he would ever know. The Greys were sorry to see him step down, but they understood that his wife's health was paramount. Dementia is a cruel disease process, and often a precursor to Alzheimer's; ultimately, Pastor Davis simply needed to step down and focus on his family.

To get the committee off to a good start, the Greys hosted a dinner at their house. They needed to discuss the different avenues available for them to find a suitable replacement—a task none of them took lightly. Justin fiddled with his smoker most of the day cooking four slabs of baby back ribs and a brisket. When Ron Winters arrived, Justin was spraying apple juice on his ribs from a spray bottle. "What on Earth are you doing? Did they get too hot and you have to cool them off?"

Justin almost laughed. "No, this is the way to finish ribs in a smoker. In fact, it's the only way to finalize the cooking process. The apple juice makes them look great and gives them a sweet finish."

Ron shook his head. "Never heard of such a thing." He sipped on his lemonade and said, "I heard something concerning you a few weeks ago I wanted to ask about."

"Whatever it is, it's probably true."

"I heard you had the nickname of Flip."

Justin did laugh. "Yep, back in high school during my football years. It's been a long time since I went by Flip."

"I'll bet there's a good story in there," he hinted.

Justin smirked. "I don't know about good, but there is a story. After homecoming my senior year we, the football team, went down by the Moyie Dam and got rip roaring plastered. All of us did. Cary Purcell raided his dad's liquor cabinet and we emptied every bottle he brought. I was so wasted I thought I could do anything. Apparently I become amorous when intoxicated and I tried to get one of the cheerleaders into my back seat. She said she would if I could do something that would impress her. One of the guys dared me to do a handstand on the hood of my car and I was afraid of being called a chicken, so I did it. When I got up on my hands, I got sick. I mean I got super sick. I started puking like there was no tomorrow. My hands slipped on the … stuff, and I went off the hood onto the ground. Legend has it I flipped a couple of times on the way down. I don't remember any of that, 'cause I hit my head and knocked myself out. The guys thought I was dead and they bolted leaving me lying there next to my car. The worst thing was when I fell I broke my leg. I had to drive myself to town to the ER. In my drunken state, I can only imagine how I made it down North Hill without driving off the mountain. I sat out the rest of the football year. The guys went on to State semi-finals, but not me. Good old Flip got a chance to lay in his vomit and nurse a broken leg." He smiled warmly. "To be honest, it's not really a nickname I liked. A few of the old guys still call me that, but I can't imagine using the name all the time. One good thing came out of the experience, though. I was so sick from the liquor that I never really developed a taste for alcohol. Well, there it is. What do you think?"

Ron was amused. "I guess we all have skeletons in our closet. Whatever happened to that cheerleader?"

"I married her."

Ron howled. "What a story. If I were you, I wouldn't go by Flip, either." He decided to change the subject. "Say, did you hear that we have a lead on a good pastoral candidate? His name is David and he is located in New Mexico."

"New Mexico? Does anything good come from New Mexico?"

"Maybe if we hire him, he will teach us how to cook chili."

"Ron, chili comes from Texas, not New Mexico."

"No, I mean red chili. You know, chili peppers. The kind where the waitress asks, 'red or green?'"

"Oh. I don't think Idaho is ready for genuine chili peppers."

Kevin joined them at the smoker. "Mom wants to know how much longer."

"Tell her I've wrapped the ribs in foil and the meat is resting."

After he had disappeared into the house, Ron asked, "So what is Kevin up to these days?"

"Well, he's busy with the Boy Scouts. In fact, he just made Star Scout. He's well on his way to becoming an Eagle. I think he has enough momentum to make it happen, too."

"Good. I always knew he'd do well. Is he still shooting?"

"Oh yeah. In fact, since I put in that rifle range in the back corner of the property, he has gotten really good. He won the 4H competition last month, and before that he took first in the NRA Youth competition down in Butte, Montana. *InSights Magazine* did an article on him that will run in the next edition."

"That's great. I didn't realize he was that good."

"He was nominated for Brownells/NRA National Youth Shooting Sports Ambassador Program, but he wasn't old enough. When he turns sixteen, he'll be eligible. The latest rumor is he's being considered for the Olympics in the Men's 50 Meter Rifle Prone team. We should know something about that soon."

Ron's eyes grew wide. "The Olympics? That's incredible. I couldn't be happier for you."

"He's a great kid. I'm glad he's found a way to excel."

"Speaking of rifles and shooting, what's the word on that indoor rifle range that you're building?

"Well, Eagle Summit will be ready in four different phases. The Bass Pro Shop and the rifle range will be the first phase, which should be finished in about two months. The second will be the Embassy Suites, the third will be the water park, and the fourth will be the indoor fishing arena."

"I still can't believe all of that is coming to Bonners Ferry. This will certainly change our little community."

"Yes, it will. Have you considered buying some land before the prices go through the roof? Land is always a good investment."

"It's too late. Land prices have exploded. A whole lot of land owners in this town are now wealthy."

"The smart ones will hold on to their property to see what they can build on it. I heard that Costco was nosing around the other day looking at land on the other side of the airport."

"Imagine that. A Costco," he said wistfully. "My wife is really hoping for a Target. And a Super Target, at that."

Justin smiled. "Someday. I think all of that will happen someday. It's only a matter of time."

"Do you think it will be successful?"

"What? Eagle Summit? I do. I think there will be no end of people coming here to have a fun-filled week. We'll need more people to work in the stores and the resort. More housing will be required. More housing means that more contractors will have to move here to build houses, which means that more gas stations will pop up, and more restaurants will arrive. We will have to hire more cops, teachers, craftsmen, and tradesmen. The school system will expand. We will see more churches start, more souvenir shops spring up, and more variety stores. This is just the beginning. Bonners Ferry is about to become a very prosperous place. Businessmen like you will soon see their profits increase significantly."

"Well, God bless America. That's all I have to say!"

Connie had just finished brushing her teeth when her cell phone rang. "Now who on earth would be calling this late?" she mused. "Connie Grey, how can I help you?"

"Is this the crisis hotline?" Her voice was barely audible.

"Yes, it is. My name is Connie, how can I help?" There was silence on the line. "Hello? Are you there?"

"Yes."

"Honey? What's wrong? Do you need help?"

"It's my mom," she whispered.

"Are your mom and dad fighting?"

"My mom's boyfriend is hitting her."

"Okay, honey? Listen to me. You must call 911. So hang up and call 911. Can you do that?"

"I did that first," she whispered, "but the deputies were on another call in Eastport. They will come as soon as they can."

Connie could hear a scream in the background and the sound of falling furniture. "Honey? What's your name?"

"Claire."

"Claire, can you get outside?"

"Yes, but I don't want to leave my mother."

"Claire, you've got to get outside for your own safety. Your mom wants that, too. So go outside and I will come to you. Where do you live?"

"At MacArthur Lake."

"I'm on my way." Justin hadn't gone to bed yet and was able to travel immediately. MacArthur Lake was only a ten-minute drive from their home. "Where are we supposed to go?"

Connie got directions from Claire as they were driving. "We've got to hurry, Justin. I can hear someone getting thrown around. It's terrifying."

"I'm going as fast as I dare considering all the deer and moose around here."

"Take the first right and then stay left at the next intersection."

"Connie, my heart is beating out of my chest and I feel jittery. I wonder if this is what cops feel every time they go on a call? I've never felt a rush of this magnitude!"

They neared the house and Justin slowed down to make sure they didn't miss the right driveway. A girl stepped into their headlights and was pointing to a narrow dirt road. He rolled down his window. "Are you Claire? Get in."

When the door closed, she pointed to the left. "The driveway splits. You have to stay to the left or you'll end up at the barn."

"How is your mom, sweetie?" Connie asked.

"I don't know. I can't hear them fighting anymore. The house is quiet."

They were almost immediately at the house. Justin left his headlights pointing at the front door. They got out but motioned for Claire to remain in the cab until the coast was clear.

"My mind is swimming. This is North Idaho, Connie!" he whispered. "Every home has guns. Every person has a gun. And we're showing up unannounced at a home where a crime was being committed. Will we be met by a man with a gun be waiting for his next victim?"

Connie stayed behind Justin as he'd insisted. *What should we do? Should we knock or just kick the door down and run through? If this was our house, I'm sure Justin would prefer the response team to knock.* As Justin gingerly lifted his fist to knock, the front door burst open and a large man stood in the doorway brandishing a knife. He was covered in blood.

CHAPTER SIXTEEN
Flip

Their trip to Boise proved uneventful but beneficial. For the first time since their lives fell apart, Ginger and Connie were able to sit and talk about everything and nothing. Ginger had always been a pleasant girl to spend time with. She liked to laugh and was quick to point out things that were funny to her.

When they were south of Lewiston, Connie asked a question she feared to ask. "Ginger, what happened? How did all of this start?"

Ginger was quiet for a long time, so much so that Connie assumed she wasn't going to answer her. Finally, she said, "At Kimee's house. Her dad gave us the pills."

Connie wanted to explode into an indignant rage but calmed herself enough for her voice to sound mostly normal. "Randy? What did he do?"

The silence was deafening. Ginger stared out the window as if she was counting the trees go by. Slowly, she started telling the story how Randy used to spend time with them and how he wanted to brush their hair. When she told Connie about Randy tricking them about being models, Connie thought she would scream. Ginger didn't talk much about the full contact abuse other than mentioning the acts occurred. She explained that Randy would give them pills to help them relax until he was through. The pills seemed to help with the pain and the embarrassment, so she kept taking them.

Connie couldn't feign stoic any longer. She pulled to the side of the road and began to cry. She thought her own life was painful, but she had no idea that Ginger was suffering an even worse fate. Ginger leaned over the console, they wrapped their arms around each other and wept for what seemed like an hour. Half a box of Kleenex later, they were able to sit up and talk some more.

"I didn't want to do drugs, Momma. But once we started, stopping was too hard. We just took the ones from Kimee's dad, but then he got arrested for drunk driving and went to jail. So we went to a guy Kimee knew at school who dealt crystal meth." She shook her head. "That stuff was horrible. They say that you can get hooked on meth from one time. I think that happened to us, 'cause we wanted more and more." Once she started talking, the whole story flooded out of her. "When we needed money to buy more, we would take things and sell them to another kid. Stuff like saws, drills, cameras, you know, small stuff that people don't notice at first."

"What did you take from me?" Connie asked.

Her lip quivered. "At first I didn't take anything. I sold my jewelry first, but then I ran out. I took some of Daddy's tools when he wasn't around to notice. The only thing I took from you was the brooch you used to wear on Sundays." She looked at her mother with wide, repentant eyes.

"So, that's where my grandmother's brooch went?" She wanted to be mad, but Ginger was being so honest, she didn't want to interrupt her. "Go on."

"Well, that's when you caught on to what was happening." Her eyes focused beyond the window again. "I'm so sorry ..."

"It's going to be okay, baby."

"I've ruined my life," she said between sobs. "What boy would want to date me? After all I did with Kimee's dad and all those videos he took of us? And all the things I stole to get high?" She gasped for air. "No one is going to want me."

Connie had no idea what to say. She just held her daughter while they wept and grieved for all they'd lost. Eventually they arrived at Boise, exhausted from their emotional drive.

"I don't want to take drugs, Momma." She said while being admitted to the rehab center. "I don't want to ever see them again. I'm going to get clean."

"I know you will, baby. And I'll be praying for you." She hugged Ginger so tight that she feared breaking her, but Ginger gave it right back. "I'm so proud of you, baby. And I will be praying."

After the heart-wrenching separation, a staff member escorted Connie to the lobby. "She has a great attitude. I expect her to get clean and remain clean. When they want to break free, they often do. I think you got to her quickly enough that a full recovery can be expected. But we need to talk about you, Connie. You need to join your local Al-Anon group and start attending those meetings. There is a whole network of people who have been there before you and who are willing to help you get through it yourself. You need to be prepared for when she is released. She'll need all of you to get back."

Connie sat in the parking lot and counted the money she had left. She had already bought gas once, and she needed to fill up again before she left. There would be one more fill up before she got home. All the gas would be around two hundred dollars out of the five hundred she had. The hour was late, and she was so tired. She wanted to spend the night before going back, but her money wasn't going as far as she hoped. If she left now, she could drive through and arrive in Bonners by three in the morning. *Maybe that will be best. Then I will have the rest of the money for my return to pick up Ginger. I'll definitely have to plan an overnight stay on that trip. Yes, it's best to drive home tonight.*

Connie stopped and picked up a burger, then started the return trip. She called Kevin to make sure he was doing okay at Chet's house. Chet was a kid who bothered her. He looked like a drug user. *Hopefully, the boys aren't smoking pot. I couldn't stand having both kids on drugs!*

How did we become the family with all these problems? We used to look out from our nearly perfect life and see those families whose kids were on drugs, or whose kids were going to jail. Now I'm trying my hardest to survive as one of those families. How did it fall apart so quickly with no place for us to hit bottom and start over?

She'd seen Flip at Zip Trip buying gas a few weeks ago. He was looking for a job as a loan officer in a bank in Spokane, but he was having trouble getting any banks to hire him. Apparently Old Man Kendall was scuttling any job in the banking industry that Flip had a chance at picking up. Flip appeared to be an entirely different man than he used to be. He had a scraggly beard and was wearing a T-shirt and shorts everywhere, which was such a stark contrast to the neatly groomed suit and tie from his former life. She knew he'd been on unemployment for many months after being fired. Then he picked up the night manager job at Super One Foods—a decent job, but not bringing in the salary he was accustomed to from the bank. It wasn't as though Connie actually cared.

That's not true, either. Flip is the father of my children and the love of my life. He certainly made it difficult to like him, though. I should call him about Ginger, but I can't stand the idea of talking to him. He still refuses to recognize what he did wrong. It still hurts me because he hasn't apologized.

The night dragged on, and she was starting to get sleepy. Connie stopped at a truck stop in Lewiston and then began the journey through the canyons that would take her to Moscow and on to Bonners Ferry. *Still so many hours!*

She was so tired her bones ached and she felt a burning in her chest that screamed at her to stop for the night, but she kept pushing on. Only four more hours. She could do it. She turned on the radio, but the only station she could pick up was Coast To Coast AM. George Norrie was interviewing a man who once lived with a family of Bigfoot in Oregon. *The story's interesting enough, but how could anyone believe … no! A deer!* Her fingers formed a death grip on the steering wheel and she involuntarily swerved to the right to avoid hitting the animal. All she could see was antlers and hooves as the deer leaped again. She struck it anyway. Her car lurched sideways into the gravel on the edge of the road. Then the screeching tires were silenced as the car rolled over and over until it came to rest just below a bridge near the edge of the highway.

CHAPTER SEVENTEEN
Justin

The man holding the knife tilted his head and looked at them as if they were ghosts. "Who are you?" he demanded. He was a large man with the early stages of a beer belly. Ironically, he was wearing a wife-beater T-shirt that was stained with fresh blood. There was blood spatter on his face. And he was glaring at Justin. "I said, who are you?"

"Ah," Justin didn't think the situation warranted an official introduction. "We're here to help. How is Tammy? Where is she?"

The man seemed confused and lifted the knife toward them. He tilted his head sideways as if struggling to understand what was happening.

Justin wanted to step back, but he held his ground. "Sir? Could you put down the knife?" He pointed to the blade. "Please? Could you drop it?"

He looked at Justin and then at Connie and then seemed to stare beyond them into the moonlit night. "Who are you people?"

Justin glanced at Connie, who said, "Ben Simpson? Are you Ben?"

He looked at her. "Who are you?"

"Ben," she said. "My name is Connie Grey, and this is my husband, Justin. We're looking for Tammy. Is she here?"

"Tammy?" the words left him like air escaping from a punctured tire. He turned away from them and stepped further into the house. "Oh my, Lord. Tammy …" He stumbled back a few feet.

Justin stepped into the room and pointed to his hand. "Ben? Drop the knife. Look at me, Ben. Drop the knife."

Ben looked at Justin through dull eyes and then seemed to register what was happening. He looked down at his hand, seemed to realize that he was holding a weapon, and then he noticed that his hands were covered with blood. "Oh, my …" He released the knife to clatter harmlessly on the wood floor.

"Ben?" Connie stepped closer to him. "Where is Tammy?"

"Tammy?" He turned and looked at the kitchen. "She's in there."

Connie pressed by him and gasped when she entered the room. "Oh, no! Justin, call 911. Do it now!"

The ambulance was long gone, but the yard was full of police cars of all shapes and sizes. Justin was still waiting on the porch for the officers to tell him that they wouldn't need to talk to him again. Connie had ridden with Claire and Tammy in the ambulance to the ER, so he was standing alone talking to her on his cell phone.

"They have stopped all the bleeding so far," Connie reported. "But she lost so much blood, they aren't sure what's going to happen. They're consulting with a surgeon to see if she needs surgery to repair some of the damage. So far, I've counted at least ten puncture wounds. This was a terrible attack."

"I wonder what would have happened if we hadn't arrived when we did? How is Claire?"

166

"She's here at the hospital sitting next to her mom's bed holding her hand. She's afraid."

"No little girl should have to endure something like that. How old is she?"

"She's thirteen. She's our kids' age."

A cold shudder ran down his back. "Man, that could have been us had God's grace not carried us so far. I can't imagine something like that happening to our kids."

"So, what happened to Ben?"

"Well, when the first officers reported to the scene, he was still covered with blood and was freely confessing that he and Tammy had been fighting and the fight got out of hand. Before he knew what was going on, he found himself stabbing her with a knife."

"What was the fight about?"

"It's so stupid. He wanted her to cook liver and onions for his dinner, but she refused. One thing led to another, and bam, Bob's your uncle."

Connie laughed. "Bob's your uncle? When did you go British on me?"

"Ever since we were drawn into watching Downton Abbey. I've been watching Midsomer Murders on iTunes while waiting for the next season to come out."

"Jolly good," she replied. "When are you going to pick me up?"

"As soon as they turn me loose. I've explained our meager part of the story several times, but never to the same person. To keep it interesting, I add something new each time I tell it."

"You're doing what?"

"Each time I tell the story, I make it a little better."

"For example?"

He thought for a moment. "Fine." He cleared his throat and then spoke as if he was in a '50s' gangster movie. "So, I knock on the door and there is Ben with this huge knife, and he points it at me, see? And I then tells him to drop it, see? And then he lunges at me, see? So I have to karate chop him, see? And then I have to tie him up, see?"

"Wow, you're in quite a mood."

"Well, it's the first time I've saved someone's life. I kind of like it."

"You're probably just giddy from lack of sleep."

"Maybe. Hold on a second, babe … Okay, I've been given the green light. I'm back on patrol."

"Well, patrol your way to the hospital and give me a ride home."

CHAPTER EIGHTEEN
Flip

Connie woke up with a flashlight probing her eyes. "She's back," a voice said from behind her. The woman with the flashlight said, "Ma'am? Can you hear me? No, you can't move your head. You'll have to speak. Can you hear me?"

"Y ... yes."

"You had a bad vehicle accident and you're at Gritman Medical Center in Moscow. My name is Dr. Harris. Do you understand what I'm saying to you? Again, honey, you can't shake your head. You have to speak."

"It ... hurts ... to ... speak."

"Okay. I'll see about that. In the meantime do you understand what I told you?"

"Yes."

"We're taking you into surgery right now. You have some internal injuries that are bleeding and we need to get that fixed. I'll come see you in recovery. Is there anyone we need to notify immediately?"

"My ... son ... but ... later. Not ... now."

"Okay. These nurses are gonna get you into the OR, so stay with us. You're gonna be okay."

When she opened her eyes, she was lying on her back in a bright room. There were no curtains drawn so she could see the activity buzzing around her. She tried to look around, but her neck didn't respond. She tried to move her hands, but they didn't respond, either. She had the same horrible luck with her feet and legs. What was happening?

She tried to speak, but a large tube was in her mouth. Her medication made her mind too foggy to properly respond or even comprehend what was happening to her. She made some coughing sounds and got the attention of a skinny, redheaded nurse who was reading the fine print on a small vial of medicine. Red Head spun around and casually said, "Hey, she's awake."

Another nurse came into view and said, "We need to remove the breathing tube before she wakes up anymore." Before Connie knew what was happening, the tube was pulled from her mouth and she was coughing. "Breathe, in and out, in and out. Concentrate on it. Come on, a little deeper now. In and out. There you go." She patted her on the cheek. "That's a good girl. You had us worried for a little while." The woman looked at her watch.

"I don't know if you remember me, but my name is Dr. Harris. Do I seem familiar?"

"Yes."

"Good. That's great. The police tell me that you hit a deer last night and rolled your car a couple of times. Fortunately, you weren't out there too long before someone noticed the wreck.

"We've got you totally immobilized right now. We were really worried that you had some spinal injuries, but I think you were lucky. If I take my pen and run it along the edge of your foot, like this … See? You have pretty good reflexes.

"We're going to keep you sedated and monitored for twenty-four hours, just to make sure everything is okay. Oh, and don't worry about your internal bleeding. We have a decent surgeon here, and he was able to stitch your spleen back together. It seems to me you're going to be okay."

While she was talking, the redhead came by and injected a medicine into her IV line. "I'll check back with you this evening. We found your son's phone number in your phone; he's been notified that you're okay and that you'll contact him tomorrow. That medicine should be hitting you right ab—"

When Connie awoke again, she was in an ordinary hospital room with a window that overlooked an air conditioning unit on the roofline on the opposite side of the building. She didn't feel bad. She didn't feel good. She wasn't feeling anything at all. And then she remembered that she couldn't move her neck or legs. But after a quick test, all of her limbs seemed to function without hesitation. She glanced around the room and saw a whiteboard on the wall that said, "Hello, Connie. Press the call button when you wake up."

She glanced around the room and realized that the call button was pinned to her gown. "I'll be right there," a cheerful voice responded without her saying anything.

A few seconds later, a young nurse with a bright smile entered the room and began fussing over her with blood pressure readings, pulse counts, and other such things. All the while she chatted away. "My name is Star and I'm the floor RN now. You're actually doing very well, considering what could have happened."

"What about my son?"

"We contacted Kevin, who is staying with his friend, Chad. He's worried about you, but we've explained to him you're okay."

"Chet."

171

"Oh, it's not that bad, is it?" Star said with a smile.

"No, Chet is his friend's name, not Chad."

"Chet. Gotcha. Anyway, at the rate you're recovering, you should be released in another day. Now, I'm going to go do some charting, but there is a very handsome policeman out here who wants to talk to you." With that, she was gone.

A tall, black-haired man wearing a dark uniform knocked sharply on the door and said, "Ma'am? May I come in?" He stepped gingerly around the corner and said, "My name is John Saddler, and I'm a Corporal with the Idaho State Police. I need to get some information about your accident."

"Won't you sit down?"

"Thank you, ma'am, but I prefer to stand. I was the one who found you on the highway—it was a pretty bad accident. Could you tell me what happened?"

She thought about it for a moment. "What I remember was a deer jumped into the road and I hit it and then I woke up here."

"Yes, ma'am, that's what happened. You swerved to miss the deer but struck it anyway. Your tires grabbed some gravel that threw your car into a series of rolls. You're lucky to be alive."

"Yep, that's me. Lucky Connie."

"Is there anything I can do for you?"

"No, sir. I can't think of anything."

"Well, I'm not going to issue you a ticket at this time. I can't see that you did anything wrong and you weren't speeding, so we'll close out that report as a no fault accident. The only thing I might add is this; next time a deer steps out in front of you, don't try to swerve. Just hit it straight on. It was the swerve that sent you into the ditch and then into the roll. Okay? Please be careful out there, Ma'am."

And with that he was gone. Connie couldn't help but compare him to Bill Sukcow but then she realized the trooper had a lot more personality.

Connie was certainly sore when released from the hospital, but she was able to function. Her surgery wasn't as invasive as she imagined and other than feeling as though she was shot out of a cannon and into a bridge, she was okay. Her insurance provided her a rental car until she could work out an agreement with her insurance adjuster. She had full coverage on her SUV, but she'd raised the deductible to the point that she couldn't afford to replace the vehicle. The adjuster agreed to write her a check for the value minus the deductible, which didn't leave her much to work with.

The days she missed from work were going to be a major problem in the weeks to come and coming up with the money to pay rent seemed impossible. She still had some cash from the church, but that wasn't going to last long. She could hardly wait until the bills from the hospital started to cycle through. The next few months were looking dismal.

When she arrived home, she had a letter from Ginger telling her that all was well in rehab. She was responding positively to the treatments and was even making friends with some of the other patients. She mentioned one girl named Mona, who was a few years older than she and was from Sandpoint. Ginger didn't know about her mother's accident and Connie preferred that she didn't find out until she was released from rehab. There was no point in Ginger worrying over something she couldn't help with anyway.

Kevin appeared glad to see his mother again but wasn't terribly sympathetic about her diminished capacity. He would get something for her if she requested it but didn't go out of his way to make her comfortable. Kevin was always the type who absorbed pain or discomfort and still pushed forward. He had a high threshold of pain and automatically assumed everyone else did as well. That was a topic Justin was working on with him before the big changes occurred.

Justin would have taken care of me and made certain that I was resting comfortably and lacking nothing. Justin was kind and compassionate. Flip, though, is hard and pushes away all of us. I have no intention of letting him know what happened to me on the trip and don't care if he ever discovers that Ginger is in rehab. He didn't care about us when things started to fall apart; he certainly isn't going to care about us now.

Connie had heard through the grapevine that Flip was seeing a new woman, and they hit it off rather well. She decided she didn't really care. Flip could do what he wants to and probably would. If he wanted another relationship—fine!

I sure don't want another relationship. Flip wounded me enough for one lifetime. As far as I'm concerned, love can stay away from me. I don't need a man in my life and I sure as heck don't want that kind of pain again. I'm happy the way I am.

But still she wondered, *what would it even feel like to be in love? Is love something that will return to me naturally, or do I have to make it happen?* She looked at herself in the mirror and didn't see a woman who was very captivating. Her hair was full of split ends and she was in desperate need of a trim. Her cheeks were sunken and her clothes were baggy. She guessed she'd lost somewhere around thirty pounds throughout the separation and divorce. She could certainly afford to put on at least ten pounds. Three or four years ago, she would have jumped for joy at losing thirty pounds, but now it seemed like a burden. *Where do I get the money to buy clothes that actually fit?* Flip was working so little that his child support payments were all but meaningless.

Well, my life isn't going to get any better while staring at a scarecrow in the mirror. I need to get to Davis to get the books done. The job isn't so bad, but working for Ben Simpson is no picnic—he sure irritates folks and pushes them away. At least he's never been rude or mean to me. It's nice having a boss who's civil to me.

The weather was cool and rainy, not untypical of North Idaho this time of year. Not untypical for her, either. The sun hadn't shown itself to her in so long, she wasn't sure if she would recognize it if it did.

The office was empty when she arrived. The first thing she noticed was the acrid smell of burnt coffee. Someone left the pot on last night and scorched the pot again. Connie figured that was no big loss, for no one came to their store for the quality of the coffee they brewed.

She set the file box she was carrying by her desk. She worked her way through the display models of hydraulic lifts and trailer hitches until she reached the coffee pot in the corner by the calendar of John Deere tractors from the 1950s. She could hear Ben tapping on his keyboard and half shouted a generic greeting to him while she poured a cup of motor oil-like coffee for herself.

"Good morning, Connie," he grunted in reply.

"Care for some coffee?"

"I already have some, thanks."

And with that pleasant exchange, she returned to her desk where she began pouring over invoices. An hour later, she needed to take a bathroom break, which irritated her to no end. She hated using the bathroom here. Theirs was a community bathroom that apparently was seldom cleaned, except for weekends when Connie worked. Once she finished that task, she stopped at the coffee pot again and then made her way to her desk.

"Connie? Before you sit down, would you take a look at this order form? I think we accidentally ordered a skid-mounted tailgate mulcher instead of the Aqua Mulcher 200."

She picked up a file and carried it and her coffee to Ben at the counter. "Is it for Crop Circle Landscaping?"

"Yes."

She glanced over the order form and then referenced her notes. "You're right—looks like a mistake. Do you want me to call and change the order?"

He ran his fingers through his short hair. "No, I'll need to let Crop Circle know that their order will be delayed. I'll take care of it."

"Okay." She turned to retreat to her desk and tripped over an adjustable stabilizer bar leaning against the counter. When her feet tangled with the drawbar, she fell headlong into a display of tractor manuals, causing the entire rack to fall on top of her. She landed with a grunt and lay flat on the ground.

"Connie!" Ben called out and rushed to her side. "Are you okay?" He pushed a stack of manuals aside and reached for her. "Stay where you are until we know if you're okay."

"Oh," she mumbled. "I think I'm okay."

"Let's make sure." He reached across her shoulder and gently rolled her to her side. "Is that okay?"

"Yes, I think so," she responded after a second.

"Let's try sitting up." Again his arms went around her and lifted her torso until she was sitting. "How is that?"

"My ankle is a little tender."

"Let's see." He knelt beside her and gently lifted her ankle into his lap. His pressed against her joints with his fingers and said, "Nothing is broken."

"I didn't realize you were a doctor."

"I was a medic in the Army. He massaged her ankle and calf for a moment. "How does it feel?"

"Tender. But it's probably just a twist." She scooted back to sit against the counter. "Maybe if I just catch my breath for a moment."

"Take your time." He smiled and the wrinkles around his eyes smiled also. "That was a nasty fall."

Connie shook her head in dismay. "And it was an embarrassing fall."

"Actually, it was kind of pretty."

That made her laugh. "Well, I've been called a lot of things lately, but pretty isn't one of them."

"I don't believe that for one minute," he said warmly. "You look pretty to me."

"Well, I …" She changed the subject. "It looks like I watered your tractor manuals with a cup of coffee."

He looked her sternly. "I wish you hadn't done that."

"Oh," she said, deflated.

"There's no call to waste perfectly good coffee like that." And then he laughed.

"Especially coffee this good," Connie noted.

"Come on, it's not that bad."

"Actually it is," she said with a smile.

"Maybe you should make the coffee."

Connie shook her head. "I would, but my boss won't let me come in any earlier. He's a stickler about the hours I keep."

"Maybe we should look into straightening your boss out, huh?"

"Maybe I shouldn't have complained about the coffee. Now I'm stuck making it."

Ben rolled to his haunches and chuckled. "My grandfather was an old cowboy who grew up ranching in Montana. He said that on their cattle drives, whoever complained about the food was the one who had to cook. He tells us that one cowboy had been stuck cooking for several days, so he put a handful of dirt into the beans to get someone to complain so he could go back to the herd. Another cowboy comes along and tastes the beans and says, 'There's dirt in my beans—but that's the way I like them.'"

The story wasn't particularly funny, but for some reason it delighted her and she started laughing along with Ben. She leaned against the counter and laughed as if she had never laughed before. After a moment of hysteria, she settled down and realized that Ben was still holding her ankle in his lap. She quickly withdrew her leg and said, "Well, I guess I should see if I can walk."

Ben helped her to her feet and smiled satisfactorily. "You don't appear to be broken."

She tested her foot. "No, everything seems okay." She put her shoe on and decided she would be okay. "I'm glad I wasn't wearing heels. These flats probably saved my life."

She and Ben busied themselves repairing the damage she'd inflicted upon the store with her acrobatics. She returned to her desk once the coffee was mopped up.

Connie tried to focus on her invoices again, but for some reason her mind kept drifting. She could still feel Ben's fingers as they caressed her ankle, massaging and probing. It had been so long since she experienced physical contact, a touch, from anyone, much less a man.

For the first time in years, she felt a flicker of warmth, a small spark of life in her soul. *How long has it been since I smiled and laughed? The story Ben told was so funny! I've never seen that side of him before. I certainly never knew him to be humorous at all. And yet he is. And he is kind, as well.*

She didn't make great progress with the books, as she kept reflecting on the bizarre experience she had with Ben. When three o'clock rolled around, she realized she had to make some progress or she would be there all night. She buried her nose in her books and scribbled away in the ledger.

She heard Ben run the closing report on the cash register and listened as he dropped coins in the till for Monday. Before she knew it, he was standing behind her. "Are you trying to work overtime?"

"I guess I'm just slow today. Maybe I'm addled from my swan dive into the display rack."

"How much more do you have to do?"

"I'm almost there. I need to take care of the payroll taxes and I can call it a day."

"Good." He turned to leave and then hesitated. "So, how are you?"

She nodded. "I'm okay. More embarrassed than injured, to be honest."

He agreed. "I know, I keep seeing you careen into that display. I was so worried that you hurt yourself."

"Aw, no need to worry about me. I'm pretty tough."

"I'll say," he said with approval. "Say, I was about to grab a bite to eat. Would you care to join me?"

"Really?" Was he asking her out? "I, uh …" She didn't know what to say.

Suddenly he was embarrassed. "No, I understand. It's okay. It's Saturday night. You probably have a hot date tonight."

"Actually, I don't." *Ha! A hot date. I haven't been on a hot date since ... college?*

"So, is that a yes, or a no?" He actually seemed interested in her. It was cute the way he was tugging on his ear while he was waiting for her answer. "It's my treat," he said hopefully.

"Hmm?" And then she realized she'd never actually responded to his invitation. "You know what, it would be fun. Let's do it." And then she realized that her statement could be misconstrued. "Let's do dinner, that is."

"Right." He pretended not to know what she meant. "How does pizza sound?"

"Ah, that sounds good. It sounds great, actually. I haven't eaten pizza in a long time."

"Goat Mountain Pizzeria?"

"Okay."

They split a pizza and a bottle of wine. Even though Ben drank most of it, Connie had enough to help her relax and enjoy the meal. He spent most of their time telling her Army stories and explaining to her why the Mud Bogs were the most definitive aspect of living in Moyie Springs. "After all," he concluded, "anytime you have a store that advertises cheap beer and good food, you can't go wrong." He laughed. "Have you ever been to a mud bog?"

"No, I can't say I have. Remember, I was married to a banker, not a lumberjack."

"Ouch," he declared. "That's unnecessary violence. The mud bog draws all kinds of people from all walks of life."

"One year," she began, "we were given tickets to the mud bog. We went out there on Saturday night and we were absolutely shocked. There were people stacked up on top of each other. We estimated there must have been close to ten thousand people out there in the middle of that field watching trucks plow through mud holes. The smoke in the air and the music blaring was a little too much for us. I figured most of the smoke came from weed."

He nodded. "Oh, I can promise you that. So, you're one of those uppity types? I figured you for a fun woman."

"Ha! I don't know where you got that idea. Have you ever seen me smile?"

The thought made him sad. "No, I guess I haven't. But it can't all be bad, right?"

"I suppose." She looked at her watch. "They're closing soon." She placed her napkin on the table.

"Well, this was nice," Ben said. "Maybe we can do it again?"

She wasn't sure what surprised her most, the fact that he wanted to go out with her again, or the fact that she was interested. "Yes, let's do."

"How about Friday night? Do you have big plans next weekend?"

Her heart sank. "I can't. I have to go to Boise and pick up my daughter. She's being released."

"Already? I can't believe the month has passed so quickly. Are you looking forward to getting her home again?"

"Yes, very much so."

"And yet you don't look too happy about it."

"No, I am. Really. It's just a hard drive down there. And I had such hard luck when I went down. And gas prices seem to keep going up. There's just a lot of stuff surrounding getting her back where she belongs. But, I'm very excited about seeing her again."

"Well, I have a great idea. Why don't we go down together? I can drive, that way you won't feel overwhelmed."

"Oh, I don't know …"

"I would enjoy the trip and I really enjoy your company. Why not?"

"It's just that I was going to spend the night, and … well …" *This is awkward,* she thought.

"I see. Let's just make it a nonstop trip then. It's a long day, but we couldn't have better company. Unless you'd rather go up, spend the night, and come home. I'll pay for an extra hotel room. I promise to be a gentleman."

Connie thought it over. *This will help me quite a bit. I have no idea where to get gas money and I really dread making this trip alone again.* "Sounds good to me."

CHAPTER NINETEEN
Justin

Justin sat in the audience with Connie and beamed with pride over Ginger's excellent performance in the drama. "That was great," he said with satisfaction.

"No, it was spectacular," Connie boasted. "They did a great job."

Justin noticed the foyer doors open. Janet approached him carrying a cell phone. When Connie saw her, she said, "Oh, not now."

Janet quietly knelt next to his chair and whispered, "It's the President. He needs you to explain something to him."

He frowned, but accepted the phone and quickly disappeared from the auditorium. Janet knowingly caught Connie's eye and offered a silent apology.

"I hope he doesn't miss the next part of the show," Connie lamented.

"It's okay," Janet offered. "The schedule says there is a ten-minute intermission while they reset the stage."

Connie nodded. The next performance was Ginger's debut as a director.

Justin returned from his phone call. "Did I miss anything yet?"

"Not yet. They're still setting the stage for Ginger's play."

"*The Sin Box*?"

"Yep, *The Sin Box*. So, how was the President?"

"Busy. One thing about taking those calls, they're generally pretty quick. He doesn't have a lot of time."

"What did he want this time?"

"He had a question about compound interest."

"What did you tell him?"

"That it is the most powerful force in the universe. He actually laughed when I said it."

"That's my husband, he entertains the President." She patted him on the leg. "Do they know that compound interest is not really your field of experience?"

"All they know is if they have a question that has any connection to financial matters, I am one of their go-to people. It's actually pretty cool."

"What? Having the President's ear? Helping shape national policy?"

"Actually, it's telling the President that I have to go because my daughter's play is about to begin."

"You're drunk with power, Flip."

He groaned. "Please, don't ever call me that again. You know how much I hate it." He grinned at her. "Oh, I have one other little tidbit of information."

"Do tell," she coaxed.

"I heard the Olympic team is being assembled …" he paused for effect.

"And?"

"And it will be announced later this week that our son is going to be on the team."

"Hah!" she squealed, causing everyone around them to gawk at her. "Our Kevin is going to the Olympics? What an honor!"

"He's worked so hard. He has a real shot at winning gold, pun intended."

"Well, pun accepted. That is just awesome. I can't wait to tell him."

Justin lifted his finger. "Uh-uh, we can't tell him."

"You've got to be kidding me."

"No. They said to keep it under our hats. They will make the announcement next Friday. We will respect that request."

"Oh, it's going to kill me. I don't think I can wait."

"Yes, you can, and you will too. Imagine how proud he will be when they call out his name. He'll feel like he won an Oscar or something."

"Or something. Something important."

"The comparison I was making was the anticipation of being selected and the overwhelming joy of hearing your name called."

"Well, then compare it to the Nobel Peace Prize, not the Oscars."

"You know the Nobel Peace Prize was conceived by Alfred Nobel, the inventor of dynamite."

"Oh, whatever."

"And as for the Olympics…"

"Not this again," she groaned. "Do you have to complain about this every time the subject comes up?"

"You know that I think the Olympics is one of the most corrupt …"

The lights dimmed. "Oh, here we go!" Connie announced. "It's show time."

CHAPTER TWENTY
Flip

Despite her apprehension about traveling to Boise with Ben, she enjoyed the journey. Half of the trip she spent venting about how things had gone wrong after Flip returned from the convention. It was probably the first time she actually spent time discussing what had happened and expanding upon how it changed their lives. Ben listened attentively and offered an occasional observation. She felt so much better getting all her problems off her chest and out into the open; she was almost a new woman.

Before long, she was able to laugh and enjoy the trip and was surprised at how much she enjoyed spending the day with Ben. "I can't imagine Ginger's face when she sees that I came with a friend."

"Is it that unusual to have a friend?"

"For me it is. Especially a man. She knows I swore to never be friends with a man again."

Ben started slowing down as they approached a road construction site. "Do you think you'll ever fall in love again?"

What an interesting question. If asked the same question a week ago, she wouldn't have bothered to respond. But now she was starting to feel alive again. She was so hungry for nurturing love that she could hardly imagine saying no. "I can tell you that I will never get married again. Period."

"Amen to that," he seconded and then scratched his nose. "Connie?"

Just hearing him say her name made her feel energized.

"I want to do something for you, but I don't want you to misunderstand. It's a big event to get Ginger back clean and sober. It's something we should celebrate. How about we extend our stay by one more night and I'll take you girls out to dinner and a movie?"

It sounded wonderful. "Gee, Ben, I don't know…"

"Come on. When's the last time you went and saw a movie?"

"More than two years ago. Maybe longer." She shook her head. "No, I have so many medical bills. I can't afford to take any time off."

He wasn't going to give up. "I'll treat you, both of you, to fresh new haircuts and a new outfit. We'll start tonight with you. You can get all gussied up and when Ginger sees you, she'll understand just how proud of her you really are."

"I don't know …"

"We have a free night anyway. We can't pick her up until morning. I'll take you down to the mall and we'll get you all set up. And then I can take you to a boot scootin' cowboy bar that I know. Doesn't that sound pretty good?"

Yes, it sounds good. I've done nothing but work and cry for so long I've forgotten what fun is all about.

After a few more tries, Ben finally got through to her.

"Yes, Ben, okay!"

He took her to Town Square Mall and, after a few minutes, they found a walk-in beauty salon. Her hair was in horrible shape from having been neglected for so long. Over time, her hair had grown long, mostly due to her lethargy. Even after the haircut, she had a lot of length to work with.

They left the beauty salon with approving looks and comments from the staff; Connie could barely contain her grin.

Ben then found the Red Lobster, where he could sit and drink beer while Connie got her nails done. *He certainly has an instinct about women and about giving us what we need.* When she returned to him, he was three beers along, and downright cheerful. Only after touring almost every dress shop in the mall did Connie find what she wanted at Kohl's. When she came out of the dressing room, Ben's mouth dropped and he was almost speechless. "My Lord, look at you! Why, you're … you're beautiful—" was all he could utter. And then he managed to say, "You've got to buy that dress. That's the one right there."

"Do you really think so?" Connie whirled around in front of the mirror like a schoolgirl. She couldn't believe she had lost almost two dress sizes, dropping from nearly a twelve to a for sure eight. That dress was made for her, and she felt transformed into a fun, new woman. Spring had come into her life, and she could hear the bluebird of happiness singing on her window sill.

Ben endured all the shopping he could handle and then insisted they find a place to eat.

"Can we go to the Cheesecake Factory?" Connie asked.

"Sure thing. Let's step on it, I'm hungry," mock-growled Ben. "You know, there is something about a newly made-over woman that makes them even more captivating than normal. They have a special swing in their steps, a snap to their fingers, and a glow about them that makes them beautiful. Connie, you're hot stuff!"

She smiled; she knew it.Ben insisted that Connie join him in a drink. After much hesitation, she ordered a strawberry margarita, which went to her head. She was a complete novice concerning alcohol, other than her disdain for martinis, and the moderate amount of tequila in her drink gave her a buzz.

She felt good. "Whee! This drink is making me tiddly!" she giggled.

"Let's go to Humpin' Hannah's for some dancing," Ben suggested. Connie was ready to try anything, and Ben didn't seem surprised to discover it was a honky-tonk night.

They weren't the oldest patrons, but they certainly stood out among the college kids who were drinking and whooping it up. In her college days, Connie could dance, and it hadn't been that long, not really, since she did some two-stepping.

She quickly discovered that she was out of shape and her legs were burning, but when Cotton-Eyed Joe played, she summoned the strength for one last line dance. Even though she was appalled at the cowboy dancing next to her, she was secretly proud that he kept running his hand over her chassis.

But chaos broke out when Ben saw the cowboy pat Connie's bottom, and he barked out, "Get your hands off my woman!" The would-be cowboy was drunk and flipped him off, but wasn't up for knuckle busting, so he stumbled to his chair and let them be. By that time, Connie was spent.

The two margaritas she drank at the bar gave her a surge of energy, but the energy didn't last long. She wasn't up for a late night.

Ben nodded. "You're too dangerous to take to a bar," he said while keeping an eye on the drunken cowboy.

She laughed gaily. "What does that mean?"

"You draw too much attention from the men," he replied with an edge to his voice.

Was he actually irritated? She couldn't tell. "I had you to protect me. I heard you tell that one kid to take his hands off your woman." She looked at him through blurry eyes. "Am I your woman, Ben?"

He had a hard look. "You were there with me."

"Are you drunk?"

"Hardly. I only drank five beers. I can still drive if that's what you want to know."

"You had five at Humpin' Hannah's, but you had a few before that."

"I can hold my liquor, don't you worry about that."

Okay. He is starting to get irritated; I don't want that. "This was fun, Ben. Thank you for taking me."

"You can thank me later," he said sweetly. "When you're ready."

When she was ready? Was he kidding? No, I don't think so. She hadn't thought about men in so long that she hadn't considered sleeping with anyone, Ben included. It had been so long … It had been a very long time, indeed.

When they arrived at their motel, Ben dutifully paid for two rooms and handed her a key to one of them. "This one is yours. I'll be right back."

"Where are you off to this late?"

"It's only ten, you know?" He pointed at the gas station across the street. "I'm going to pick up a six pack." He looked her over and grinned devilishly, which sent a thrill down her spine. "Would you like to walk with me?"

She considered his offer. "I could use some fresh air."

He found the six pack he wanted and some wine coolers that she thought looked tasty. They returned to her room, where he sat in the only chair in the room while she leaned back against the headboard. Ben drank several of the beers while they watched *The Late Show*. When it was time for him to call it a night, he lingered by the open door until she joined him. It had been a wonderful night. She was feeling good. Really good. And, even though she knew she would regret it, she pulled Ben back into the room and closed the door. His plan had worked.

When morning came, she found herself slightly hung over, but not too bad. Her hangover was nothing compared to the shock of waking up with a man in her bed.

What did I do? I can't believe I slept with him. What was I thinking? Just because he swept me off my feet with the wonderful attention and the much-needed pampering? I really got caught up in the moment. But, oh I wish I hadn't done it. She took an extra-long and hot shower and tried to wash his cologne off of her skin. *What have I done? I wanted him last night, but I sure don't now. And I still have to ride back with him to Bonners Ferry. It's going to be a long day. Talk about awkward!*

Thankfully, when she got out of the shower, Ben was in his own room getting ready, and she sat on the bed in bewilderment. What had gotten into her? She would never have done such a thing in the past. Even in college she was pretty conservative. She and Justin didn't carry on like that, and she didn't approve of that kind of behavior. She wasn't the kind of woman to engage in a one-night stand. Was her pain so intense that she was this vulnerable?

Another thought horrified her and made her feel cheap. *Did Ben manufacture this entire event just to get me into bed? Am I that naïve? How dare he take advantage of me? I should be furious!* She needed time to pull herself together. She sat on her bed and tried to cry, but the tears weren't available. To make matters worse, *I really did have fun last night. I enjoyed the evening with Ben, and I enjoyed spending time with him here in this very bed. I know it's wrong, but our love-making thrilled me. I'm so confused.*

Why didn't sin feel like sin until the deed was done?

When Ben returned, he had a box of donuts and chocolate milk, one of her favorite breakfast meals. She dreaded looking at him, but once she saw his smile and his eyes, she knew she wasn't angry. When he touched her cheek gently and brushed her hair behind her ear, she felt her heart melting again. She needed some time. She needed some space. She needed to think—even to pray.

She wanted to despise him, but then he said, "You're even more beautiful this morning." He handed her a donut. Chocolate covered. "When I first saw you come into the shop looking for a job, I knew there was something special about you. I knew you were an incredible woman. But I figured I didn't have a shot at being with you. You seemed so … above me, so out of my reach." He drank from his milk bottle. "I'm just a clumsy, backward clod who doesn't deserve a break and then you come into my life."

He looked down at the floor and said, "And I owe you an apology. I didn't want to take advantage of you. You were so tempting, so desirable, and so beautiful that I was blind with passion. I won't hide the fact that I am already falling for you, but I didn't want it to happen like this. I wanted our first time to be … different. So, if it's okay with you, let's try to put this behind us. Let's try not to focus on last night. Let's just take a step back, 'cause I need time to think. I want you more than I've ever wanted a woman, but I want it to be right. So, let's just slow down and let me pursue you the right way. What do you say?"

Why did God design women to need love, comfort, and strength from a man? And why did He make men need sex? What a complicated mess this situation with Ben has turned out to be. She determined to not think about it and focused on getting Ginger back into her life.

"I missed you so much, baby," Connie said while chatting with her on the way home. "I've been worried about you."

"I missed you too." She was watching Ben, who was adjusting the radio. She couldn't believe that her mother came with a man and was suspicious that more was happening between them than hanging out as friends. But, when Connie told her about her accident and subsequent hospitalization, she understood how Ben came along for the journey. The more she watched him, the less she liked him. In many ways, he reminded her of Kimee's dad, Randy. He had a way of looking at her and Connie that made her feel dirty. And he seemed angry and unapproachable. What did her mom see in him?

"So," Connie asked. "What's the biggest thing you learned at rehab?"

Ginger smiled and said dutifully, "If it brings harm to none, do as you will."

"What does that mean?"

"It's kind of like Karma, Mom. It's called the Rede."

"They teach Karma at rehab?"

"Not really. I got that from Mona, my friend from Sandpoint. She helped me out a lot. Most of the stuff she talked about really helped me realize I wasn't just hurting myself, but I was hurting others. Like when I stole your brooch or Daddy's tools. I was hurting my friends and my family."

"Well, Mona sounds very wise," Connie replied.

"And she taught me how to be more in tune with nature and to find solace and meaning in it."

Connie looked at her carefully. "That sounds very New Agey."

"Maybe a little. But what I was doing was not good and I think that by finding more harmony and meaning in nature, I can find more of those things in my own life. I don't want to be the same anymore. I no longer want to be the Ginger, who was a victim. I want to live my life, love myself, and love others."

Connie was concerned with Ginger's new philosophy. She should be turning her heart toward God, Who could heal her and make her whole again. But as she thought that, she chided herself, *who are you to tell her to seek God? You, yourself are not walking with Him, why should you tell her to do the same thing? That's hypocrisy.* She finally said, "That sounds very positive. It seems to me you have a pretty good plan that will help you stay on track." *There*, she thought. *That's a very middle of the road thing to say.*

"When Mona gets released, we're going camping. I'm really looking forward to it."

Connie watched Ginger as her eyes sparkled and as she spoke with such optimism. *She's no longer my little girl; she's so very much a woman. I'm just so sorry she's lost her innocence and that sense of wonder. My baby girl is all grown up!*

When they got home, Connie was greeted with a message on her answering machine that Kevin had gotten into another fight and seriously injured a boy. Therefore, she was summoned to an important parent/teacher conference as soon as possible.

What am I going to do about Kevin? He's becoming more aggressive every month. I bet Chet is the reason Kevin is fighting so much. Chet's forever teaching him how to perform karate-type moves and they're breaking boards in the back yard with kicks and punches. I thought martial arts taught their students to seek peaceful paths and to only use their skills in defense, not aggression. Then again, Kevin wasn't under the instruction of a sensei, but rather under the influence of Chet, the boy who couldn't find a way to stay in school without getting in trouble. The two of them together certainly seemed to be a classic example of the blind leading the blind.

Connie was excited. She and Ginger had a special day planned. The two of them were going to share a wonderful meal at Forty One South, a steakhouse on the edge of Lake Pond Oreille where the long bridge crossed the crystal clear water of the magnificent mountain lake. She hadn't seen Ginger in many months as she and Mona had moved in together in Sandpoint and were inseparable. As she entered the restaurant and explained to the hostess that she was meeting her daughter, she saw Ginger sitting on one of the outdoor dining terraces that spilled down to the edge of the water. Ginger jumped out of her chair when she saw her mother approaching. "Yay, you made it!"

"Of course, I made it. I'm your mother, for Heaven's sake."

They shared small talk until the waitress came and took their order. Ginger insisted that she order the filet mignon, one of the signature steaks of superior quality. The meal was Ginger's treat, so Connie agreed and greatly pleased her daughter.

"So, how's Kevin?"

Connie sighed. "About the same. His probation officer tells me that he's destined to spend some time in the pen if he doesn't settle down. I really don't know what to do with him. It seems that every time I try to talk to him, he just becomes more problematic. His father can't seem to get through to him, either."

"He's so hard-headed."

"And it doesn't help that he keeps flirting with his probation officer. I keep reminding him he's only going to make her mad. She's a mother of three and is happily married, but does he care? Nope. He seems oblivious to the fact that her husband would rip his head off, but he's a teenager. You can't tell him anything."

"How are Grandma and Grandpa?"

Connie exhaled slowly. *I'll take Difficult Topics for $500, Alex*, she thought. *Is this the day when Ginger drags me through all the dirty laundry?* "Well, you know that they haven't been supportive of us in this entire matter from the day your father and I separated. Which was all my fault, of course."

Ginger rolled her eyes. "Yep, and you can imagine how they reacted when they found out that I was using drugs. They haven't talked to me since. They're the people who make Christianity ugly. So, you haven't heard from them?"

Connie shook her head. "Oh no. They won't even take my calls. When Ben and I started dating, my mom told me I was a Jezebel and I deserved whatever happened to me."

"I'm sorry about that. I know why Dad left, and it wasn't your fault." Ginger sliced some bread for her mother and mercifully changed the subject. "I did invite you here because I wanted you to celebrate with me. Can you believe I've been out of rehab for one year and one day?"

"Really? It doesn't seem like it."

"So much has happened in the last year, Mom. You and Ben are living together, but why, I certainly don't know."

Connie swallowed hard. "Ginger, don't start with me. You don't know Ben as I do. He's a good man; he's just rough around the edges."

"He's mean, Mom. He yells at you and I suspect he might even hurt you."

Her anger flashed. "That's not true, Ginger. You know better."

Ginger smiled warmly. "But I didn't bring you here to fight, I just wanted to celebrate. Since Dad moved off to North Dakota, you're the only parent I have left." She slathered butter on her bread slice. "So … there's something I wanted to share with you, but I'm worried that you'll overreact."

"Wow. That sets the stage rather ominously."

"I just wanted you to be prepared and to be supportive."

"I've been warned, and I will be supportive. You know I'm your mother, after all. No matter what, I'll always love you."

"Ah, I love you too, Mom." She batted her eyes.

"Is this where you tell me you're gay?"

Ginger blushed. "No, you already knew that, didn't you?"

Connie shrugged. "I certainly suspected it a while back. You aren't very good at hiding the truth. But, I've been waiting for you to actually tell me."

"It's true," she said casually. "Mona and I are very happy too."

"Speaking of Mona, where is she?" Connie asked tersely.

"She's working late, but will join us for dessert."

"Great," she said with a lack of enthusiasm. "So, what is the big news? I'm ready for anything."

"Okay, here goes …" She was nervous and her laugh made it obvious.

"Ginger, relax," Connie soothed her. "What can you tell your parent that's more surprising than you're gay? Just spit it out."

"You're right. So, I'm just going to say it." She began again. "For the last year and a day, I've been in the broom closet."

"The broom closet? What's that?"

"I've been studying Wicca."

"What?" Connie was wrong; there was an announcement that was more surprising than your daughter declaring she's gay.

"I've decided to worship the Earth and I now serve the god and goddess."

"You what?"

"You know, Karma and the Wiccan Rede, right?"

Connie was stunned. "No, I don't know. What're you talking about?"

"Well, I'm now worshiping the creation rather than the Creator. I even have a closer relationship with my god than you or other Christians probably do with yours. My god and goddess need me and I need them. Jesus made it very clear that He doesn't need us, but we need Him."

"What?" She couldn't believe what she was hearing.

"I now practice magick and I cast spells."

"You're doing what?"

"In my coven, we practice magick."

"Coven?" Connie shook her head. "You're a devil worshiper now?"

Ginger laughed calmly. "Not at all. That's a very common misunderstanding. Wiccan religion doesn't even teach about Satan, that's only in Christianity, Judaism, and Islam. We no more worship Satan than you do. Satanism and Wicca are as different as Christianity and Atheism."

Connie's eyes were glassy. "Is this because you're gay?"

"Mom, don't be silly. It's true Christianity has a negative and restrictive view of sex and sexuality, but Wicca regards responsible sexual behavior as a gift of the goddess. Some committed Wiccan couples engage in private sexual rituals. But all sexual orientations are normal and natural."

"Did Mona drag you into this?"

"Really, Mom. I haven't been dragged into anything. Mona just helped me figure out what I wanted. I don't want to overwhelm you, but I wanted to respect you enough to explain what was going on with me. I think Margot Adler said it best:

> *We're not evil. We don't harm or seduce people. We're not dangerous. We're ordinary people like you. We have families, jobs, hopes, and dreams. We're not a cult. This religion is not a joke. We're not what you think we are from looking at T.V. We're real. We laugh, we cry. We're serious. We have a sense of humor. You don't have to be afraid of us. We don't want to convert you. And*

please don't try to convert us. Just give us the same right
we give you—to live in peace. We're much more similar
to you than you think."

Connie closed her eyes and leaned back in her chair. What was happening? How had their lives come to this? She heard rustling behind her and lifted her hand. "Waitress? I'd like to order a martini …"

CHAPTER TWENTY-ONE
Justin

Kevin stood over the shoulder of a boy staring intently down a rifle barrel. "Line up your sights and keep them aimed at center mass. Once you have the sight picture you want, exhale slowly, and then gently squeeze the trigger. You should be squeezing so gently that the shot should almost surprise you." The rifle recoiled with a sharp BANG! The boy looked over the rifle barricade and tried to see if he hit the mark. Kevin lifted his spotting scope and announced, "Bulls-eye! Great shot. I think you're a natural."

The boy was wide-eyed with adoration. "Thank you, Kevin. That was awesome!" The boy made an effort to shake his hand. "Can I see your gold medal now?"

Kevin laughed. "Yep, just like I promised. It's in the display case."

"Can we take it out? I'd like to wear it."

"Sorry, Champ. The medal has to stay in the case. But if you want to try one on, I suggest you work really hard and join the Olympic Team."

"I will!" The boy turned to run away, and then asked, "Can I hold your Olympic rifle?"

Kevin grinned at him. "I'll tell you what, after everyone has gone through the line, I'll get the rifle out of the case and let your whole class look at it."

"Awesome!"

Kevin patted him on the head and turned to the line of students. "Okay, who's next?" Since becoming the Shooting Pro at the range, his popularity with the local school kids had grown to near rock star levels. He enjoyed teaching them to shoot and was continually surprised he was so popular. People came from far and wide to take a picture with the Olympian and his gold medals, and he'd even created his own line of shooting apparel and equipment. His signature .22 long rifle was the most popular selling long arm in the store. Technically, he wasn't out of high school yet, but as he was homeschooled, he was able to move through his studies so fast that he was graduating a full year ahead of his peers.

When the indoor facility opened the previous fall, his father never considered any other choice than Kevin to be the face of the range. Kevin was swept into national attention by setting the record for the men's 50 Meter Rifle Three Positions with an astounding 1304 points— an almost perfect score. With the 50 Meter Prone, he shot a score of 708, one point short of the maximum 709. He also scored 145 with both Trap and Skeet. His was the best showing of an American in the history of Olympic shooting events. He certainly came home to a hero's welcome. Having Kevin be the face of the range guaranteed that the indoor range was a success.

Kevin didn't intend on being the pro at Eagle Summit forever. His desire was to enlist in the Army, but he was too young when he finished his schoolwork, so he decided to stay on for a year at the resort. The Bass Pro Shop in Bonners Ferry sold more firearms than any other store in the nation, a fact that was attributed to Kevin. But Kevin insisted that the record sales were due to the ability to test-fire the long arms and pistols before buying them. Either way, the combination created an enormously successful business.

Eagle Summit was such a smashing success and had been named the "Most Improbable Success Story in History" by the *Wall Street Journal*. The business world had dismissed Justin and Grey Matters as the biggest lunatics in the Western hemisphere, but they changed their tune when Eagle Summit became one of the top vacation destinations in the United States. Eagle Summit was so successful that Six Flags Entertainment Corporation wanted to expand to Bonners Ferry and successfully secured enough property to begin construction on the new amusement park.

The biggest drawback to Bonners Ferry being the new entertainment capital of the Inland Northwest was the lack of sufficient airports. In the beginning, all air travel routed through Spokane, but, after a tremendous effort, Grey Matters succeeded in building an airport between Bonners Ferry and Sandpoint that could accommodate the volume of travelers.

The second biggest drawback was the lack of workers available to fill the positions created by the surge of businesses opening. Justin worked with Boise State University to open a branch in Bonners Ferry, which he expected to announce the next month. The university would help bring in enough college students to provide suitable employees for most companies.

Several universities were seeking Kevin as a potential recruit and aggressively offered him scholarships and various perks to secure his attendance. He spent several months considering his options with his parents and then made a decision. He was Army-bound. He also wanted to go to college. He sat down with a recruiter and they formed a plan that satisfied him. He wanted to use his skills as a marksman with the goal of becoming a sniper. He would enlist in the Regular Army as Infantry.

While he was there, he would seek to attend Basic Airborne Course and to attend the Ranger Training Brigade if he did well enough in boot camp. If he were able to stand out enough to win a slot with the Army Sniper School, one of the most physically and mentally demanding courses in the Army, he might serve in one of the most challenging and difficult duty positions in the Infantry. He would then attend college after his four-year enlistment when he would be free to pursue an academic degree without distractions.

To no one's surprise, he was the kind of recruit who stood out above his peers, but in a positive way. Anyone who had the focus and discipline to become an Eagle Scout and to compete in the Olympics would be a natural fit for the trials of being a soldier. The Drill Sergeant cadre at the 2nd Battalion, 54th Infantry Regiment, watched him carefully and focused much of their efforts to prove him as a candidate for the demanding position. Despite all their efforts to test him, he excelled and earned their respect. He was chosen to attend paratrooper training and once he earned his Airborne tab, he was given the opportunity to try his luck with the Rangers. The intense boot camp training from the thirteen weeks of infantry school, followed by the three weeks of Airborne, followed by sixty-one days of Ranger training made his physical body work as hard as his mental focus. But, as always, he dug deep into his heart and found the strength to press onward. By the time he finished Ranger school, he'd received his orders and was excited to be assigned to 2nd Battalion, 75th Ranger Regiment, in Fort Lewis, Washington, which kept him fairly close to home. He could make the drive from Seattle to Bonners Ferry in roughly six hours.

His parents proudly attended each of his Graduations from Basic, Airborne, and Ranger schools, and they were just as relieved to discover that he was to be stationed in Washington. A few months after his arrival, he received word that he was going to sniper school. So, he was back on a plane to Fort Benning, Georgia, where he had spent almost a year in training already. He found the sniper school to be just as demanding as anything else he had attempted. The mental component of sniping was surprising to him, and the patience required was a necessity. He didn't take long to realize being a good shot at sniper school was only about twenty percent of the program. The rest was spent in learning to use cover and concealment, finding the range of a target, observation skills, and finding and stalking a target. He had found his place in life. He enjoyed working alone and didn't mind digging into a hillside and waiting for a target, even if it took days.

Being assigned to a regular Ranger Battalion was an honor for him, and he was glad when his unit received orders to Afghanistan, where he had the opportunity to put his skills into battle. He never imagined what his first enemy engagement would bring.

Kevin and his spotter, Corky, were on point after they'd been called to the location where a helicopter had been downed. Instead of an easy pick up of survivors, they were engaged in a full-blown firefight.

Kevin and Corky both received the Bronze Star for their actions that day along with a Purple Heart. Kevin tried to refuse the Purple Heart because he'd been injured as a result of friendly fire, but his commanding officer dismissed his concerns with, "You received sutures as a result of combat. Enough said. You're gettin' it; you don't have to wear it."

His award read,

> By direction of the President, the Bronze Star Medal with V Device is presented to Specialist Kevin E Grey, United States Army:
>
> For heroism, not involving participation in aerial flight, in connection with military operations against a hostile force in the Republic of Afghanistan. Specialist

Grey distinguished himself by exceptionally valorous action while serving as a sniper with 2nd Battalion, 75th Rangers. Specialist Grey continually exposed himself to enemy fire during the attack and saved many possible friendly casualties by providing suppression fire against enemy combatants more than 900 meters from his position, having a confirmed thirteen kills. Specialist Grey continued effective fire at the enemy even after being wounded by shrapnel. His display of personal bravery and devotion to duty is in keeping with the highest traditions of the military service and reflects great credit upon himself, his unit, and the United States Army.

CHAPTER TWENTY-TWO
Flip

Flip had been working in North Dakota for more than a year as an operational accountant for a wildcat drilling company. He'd tried to return to the banking industry after being fired, but Old Man Kendall had spread the word about him and successfully scuttled his career in investment banking. He was lucky to get the accounting job as it required experience in the oil field industry. However, he was able to demonstrate that money management was his forte and he was given the job on a conditional basis.

He hated living in North Dakota and he especially hated his first winter. He thought living in North Idaho had given him plenty of cold weather experience, but he discovered quickly the cold in North Dakota was nothing like home. In Bonners Ferry temperatures drop below zero, but not much below zero and the cold snaps seldom last more than a week or two, and then the temperatures return to the twenties and thirties. But in North Dakota, the temperature in January didn't even make it to ten. The worst part was the wind. Bonners Ferry rarely had wind that cut through you like a knife, sending the wind chill well below zero for what seemed like weeks at a time.

His social life was strained as well. His girlfriend, Erica, lived with him for several months, but when her husband was paroled, she returned to him. Flip spent the next three months avoiding her jealous husband for fear of being pummeled.

He was on and off cocaine, depending on what was happening in his life at the moment. He could afford to use it recreationally and Erica introduced him to guy she knew who would deliver it in a pizza box. When Erica's husband violated his parole, she returned to Flip and now his social life was back in order. She was loads of fun and she loved to sing karaoke. She didn't compare to Dahlia, but then who did? She didn't cook or clean, but it wasn't a big deal because they ate takeout almost every day. He must have been addicted to Chinese food because he seemed to crave it daily.

Not long after moving to North Dakota, he began to miss home but it was always stressful when dealing with his family. His kids seemed to lay a guilt trip on him for never being around, and Connie was always piercing him with her dagger eyes. The last time he saw his son, Kevin threatened to break his nose. Kevin came to stay with Flip for a short time, exploring the possibility of moving there because he was having trouble staying in school because of his fighting.

Kevin was only enrolled in his new school for two weeks when he was suspended again. This time the police came and arrested him for assault, but the charges were dropped when Kevin promised to leave North Dakota and never return. Kevin turned on his dad when Flip made the comment he was really glad he spent all that money for bedroom furniture now that Kevin was going back to Bonners. For a moment, he thought Kevin would hit him, and was relieved when he got into his car and left. He hadn't had contact with him since.

He was troubled when he received a wedding announcement in the mail from Ginger, who was going to marry her soul mate, Mona, in a private ceremony in Colorado. He kept looking at their photo. "Too bad Mona is being wasted playing for the wrong team," he mumbled. *I really like her jet-black hair and Celtic tattoos. Well, if Ginger is happy, who am I to judge? I've made plenty of mistakes in my life. I'm sure not going to impose a stuffy moral standard on her. She's young, and you should make your mistakes when you're young, not when you're old like me*, he thought.

He certainly acknowledged his own mistakes. *Marrying Connie was the worst thing I could have done. We were so young and so inexperienced and we simply had no idea what we were getting into. I can't remember ever having a happy moment with her. She's always hounding me about something or making me out to be a loser. No, we've never been happy. I sure can't imagine living the rest of my life with her.*

I'm sure of one thing. I'm never gonna get married again. I won't repeat that mistake for any woman on the planet. Besides, I'm not the type to settle down. I'm a bachelor at heart—a wandering soul. I probably have Gypsy somewhere in my bloodline.

Yep, he was living the dream in North Dakota. It was probably the best thing he'd ever done.

Connie was brooding at her teller window, which caused her coworkers to walk a wide berth around her. Finally, Haley asked her what was wrong and she tersely replied she had a bladder infection or a urinary tract infection and she was in pain.

Haley placed a concerned hand on her shoulder. "Well, no wonder," she said softly. "You've been under tremendous stress lately with Ginger getting married, and all."

"And all" was right. Connie had grieved when Ginger rejected her Christian faith and professed devotion to the goddess.

"I know this doesn't really help, but I know a family whose son rejected his faith as well. He started following something called Jediism, which is supposed to be some kind of Star Wars or Star Trek thing. Anyway, he even walks around with a hood on all the time and even got kicked out of Silverwood Theme Park for refusing to take it off."

"That definitely seems like a problem I wouldn't want in my life," Connie replied casually.

"Anyway," Haley continued. "You should take some kind of booster and get your immune system back up. I mix my own acacia berry and huckleberry smoothies, and I put turmeric in mine as well. Just make sure it's completely organic. And nitrate free." Haley went on about making proper smoothies, but Connie really didn't care. Her infection was bothering her so much she was hardly able to concentrate. She couldn't afford it, but she had to go to the doctor.

The year following her accident had been horrible. Her insurance didn't pay much of the bill, and she was in debt up to her ears with Gritman Medical Center in Moscow. At first, she could manage the load by shuffling the payment dates, but as more bills continued to come in, she was unable to navigate that minefield. She expected the billing from the hospital, but when the individual doctor bills came, and she couldn't even remember seeing that particular doctor for anything, well, it was more than she could handle. She thought when Flip finally went back to work his child support payments would help, but it simply wasn't enough.

She and Ben continued seeing each other after their trip to Boise. She kept telling herself Ben was bad news, but she enjoyed having another human, any human, touch her, hold her hand, or hug her. She didn't realize she had been starving for that kind of affection until she received it, and then she had trouble going back into a self-induced famine.

I know Ben is wrong for me, but he's the only man who's noticed me—I just don't have the energy to look for another one. He's not all that bad; maybe a little jealous now and then, but ... I just need to be careful about talking to other men. He doesn't seem to mind my coworkers, but man, if any of the farmers pay attention to me at Davis, I sure hear about it later!

At the moment, her biggest trouble was financial. Once the debt snowball hit, she knew she had to do something or she would be destroyed. She got so far behind with her other bills while trying to handle the hospital payments she couldn't stay above water any longer. One day she mentioned to Ben she had no choice but to find a cheaper rental house and he offered a solution to a desperate situation.

If she moved in with him, then she wouldn't be paying rent, which would help her significantly. *I hate the idea. Maybe I enjoy having a man in my life on a limited basis, but moving in with him is too much like getting married. If we had a spat, Ben could toss me out, and then where would I go?* She resisted the idea of moving in with him for another month. When she realized more than half of her bills were about to be sent to a collection agency ... *Well, I have to do something. It's bank policy I have to stay current with my bills. If any bills are sent to a collection agency, they reserved the right to fire me.* The bank justified that by pointing out how tempting it was to work with large sums of cash if you were in financial distress. The temptation to steal some of it might be more than the employee could stand. *I could both move in with Ben and keep my job, or I could lose my job and lose my house. I feel trapped. None of my options is good. Is Ben really that bad?*

Kevin was adamantly opposed to moving to Ben's house, but he agreed to try it out to keep an eye on his mother. He didn't trust Ben and wanted to be there to protect her if necessary. It worked okay for a month, but Ben made life difficult for him while Ben and Connie were getting along without major conflict. However, the next time Kevin was suspended for fighting, Ben ordered him out of the house, and he was off to North Dakota, where things would be hopefully better with his dad.

When Connie came home from work and discovered Kevin was gone, she was furious. "You don't have the right to kick my son out of the house."

Ben temper flashed, and he threw his dinner plate at her. Even though it didn't come close to hitting her, she was still alarmed.

"Oh, Connie! I'm so sorry! You know I didn't mean to hurt you. But, you made me so mad. If you hadn't made me mad, I wouldn't have thrown anything." He shook his head in shame. "I'm so sorry! Won't you please forgive me? Give me another chance?"

Connie forgave him. It would never happen again.

And it didn't happen again. Not until she burnt his dinner, that is. Ben had a fascination with liver and onions and insisted Connie cook it for him at least once a week. She hated liver, and the very smell of it violated her in ways she couldn't describe. She almost gagged while preparing it, and lost her appetite completely while cooking, which offended Ben greatly.

"I'm the only one who's putting dinner on the table," he snapped at her. "Is it too much to ask that you eat dinner with me?"

"I've tried," she pleaded. "I just can't eat liver."

"That's because you always burn it! How can you develop a taste for it if you don't cook it right?"

"I'm sorry, Ben. I've tried to eat it, but I can't. I'll cook it for you, but I won't eat it."

"Well, you aren't going to eat anything else, then. You'll go hungry before I provide you two meals. You should show some respect to me for providing you food."

"Ben, I'm grateful to you. But eating liver makes me gag. You know I almost throw up trying to swallow it."

He was furious. "That's because you can't cook it right. It's not supposed to be shoe leather." He cut a slice and stabbed it with his fork. "Here, eat this. That's the only way you'll learn to like it. That's the way my father taught me, and that's the way you'll learn. Come on, eat it."

Connie was shocked. *Is he serious?* "You know I can't eat that."

His eyes were on fire. "You will eat it, and you will like it."

"No, Ben, I can't. I just won't have anything to eat at all, if that's what you want."

"What I want is for you to eat this liver. Now open your mouth and eat it."

Ben's anger frightened her. "Ben, please…"

"Open Your Mouth!" he roared. "Do It, Do It Now!" He stood from his chair and leaned over her. "You'll take it, or I'll force it down your throat."

She tried to open her mouth, but she started crying, which sent him over the edge. "Stop it, Connie. Just … open … your … mouth," he said through clenched teeth. He grabbed her jaw with his other hand and forced her mouth open.

"Ah! Ben, you're hurting me …" but the bite was in her mouth.

"Now chew it."

She wanted to comply if for no other reason than to make him stop. She bit into the liver, but the flavor revolted her and she involuntarily gagged. She steadied herself and chewed again, but it was no use. The bite came out and it wasn't alone. She spewed over her plate. That's when Ben slapped her.

When Ben struck her, he fell at her feet, apologized, and the next morning he went to Safeway and bought her flowers before she got up. That evening he made up to her, but Connie lacked enthusiasm for his affections.

"I'm really sorry, Connie. I didn't want to hurt you; you just made me so angry. Why would you provoke me like that? I love you so much, but you needed to learn to respect me. I only asked one thing of you, to eat liver with me. Was that too much to ask? Just that one thing. But, it doesn't matter. I'll never hit you again. I promised you, and I mean it. Never again. No matter how angry you make me, I'll never lay another hand on you again."

Connie was sorry, too. *I know Ben doesn't ask much of me—he's just got this hang up about liver and onions. I guess if that's the only thing he wants, I'll learn to eat it without heaving. He's been so good to give me a place to live—and he gives me everything I need. I will try to show him more respect.*

"Connie?"

"Hmm? What?"

Haley was still talking to her, and Connie's mind had drifted off, thinking about her own problems. "I'm sorry, I'm very distracted today."

"That's okay. Here, I wrote down my instructions for making a proper smoothie."

Connie looked over the list. "You put coffee in your smoothie?"

Haley smiled. "No, of course not. That would be silly. The thing with the coffee is my instructions on how to do a proper coffee enema. A really good coffee enema will cleanse your colon and flush out any toxins you're holding on to. It will make you feel like a brand new person."

Connie didn't have the energy to make a smart remark about the enema. "Thank you, Haley. You shouldn't have gone to all that trouble."

"A couple of weeks and we'll have that bladder infection cleared up." She mercifully left Connie when a new car arrived at the drive-through window.

I've got to see a doctor. I don't care what it costs. This pain is incredible. If I can just make to lunch, I can walk into Bonners Ferry Family Medicine. She always enjoyed visiting the small doctor's clinic as the staff made visits as pleasant as possible. They certainly treated her like a family member in the many years she had trusted them with her medical needs.

When she checked in, the receptionist was glad to see her. "Hey, Connie! Long time no see. What brings you here? I hope you're okay."

"I think I have a bladder infection. Can I walk in without an appointment?"

She nodded. "I'll fit you in. It's not that busy at the moment. If you'd come an hour earlier, you would have waited for a long time. So, how have you been?"

She felt better chatting and she enjoyed catching up on old times. Before long, she was called to go back. The nurse handed her a cup and asked her to fill it up so he could check to see if she had an infection.

A knock on the door after her exam told her they had results from her tests. "Well, you don't have a bladder infection."

Connie shook her head. "Then it must be a urinary tract infection."

"Actually, no. And I'm so sorry to say … you have contracted herpes."

CHAPTER TWENTY-THREE
Justin

While relaxing on the patio at Pinehurst, Gerald sat in the sunlight and lifted his tea glass in a salute to Connie. "You make the best iced tea. I'd swear I was back in the South."

"Thank you, Gerald. That is Southern tea. I always have Justin pick up a few boxes when he's in South Carolina."

"And boiled peanuts when I'm in Florida," Justin added with a smile. "And Leal's salsa when I'm in Texas."

"And turkey sausage. Don't forget the turkey sausage," Connie grinned. "Texas has a lot to offer."

Gerald laughed. "Texas is built upon barbecue, how did you narrow your choice down to just one type of sausage?"

"We make our own brisket and ribs here." Justin pointed at his smoker. "The only thing I don't care to tackle is sausage, much less turkey sausage. I've tried making it, but it's a little too … involved for my comfort."

"And where is this sausage?"

"Llano. And you have to deliberately make a trip to Llano because you aren't going to just pass through. I can never remember the name of the restaurant. It's 'something' Kitchen, and the 'something' is somebody's name. They have a big sign next to the road that says *PIT BAR-B-Q & CATERING*, and they have a big gobbler painted on the sign with a caption saying, *HOME OF TURKEY SAUSAGE*. It truly is the best around."

"Why didn't you get them to put in a branch in Bonners?" He chuckled, "You've gotten everything else up here."

"Believe me, I've tried. He just won't relocate. His is a local business, and that's that. So, it's a treat to get it when we can."

"What brought you to Llano?"

Connie refilled his tea glass. "A few years ago the kids and I wanted to go to a rodeo, so we talked Justin into driving to Texas. Also, there were a few colleges Ginger wanted to check out."

"Visiting the colleges I understand, but they have rodeos around here."

"We wanted to see an authentic Texas rodeo. Everything is bigger and better in Texas, right? Well, we drove down to Texas. We stopped at a gas station in Lubbock and asked the guy next to us what the best way was to get to San Antonio. He was a really helpful man, and the first thing he told us was it was called San-tone. Apparently you have to squish all the letters together to say it as a Texan would. He told us he recommended taking a tour of the Hill Country, and he mentioned a few towns, Kerrville, and Fredricksburg. And then he said if we went that way, to stop in at Llano and eat some truly magnificent pit BBQ. So we did. And it was great," she said with a wide smile. She glanced at her husband. "You know, we still have some in the freezer. We may have to warm it up to share with Gerald."

"Yes, that's what we need to do."

Gerald protested, "Not on my account."

"No, now that we're talking about it, we have to do it. I'm hungry for it. Besides, Connie's already gone to get it." He watched his wife saunter away from him and his heart smiled.

"You drove all that way for a rodeo?"

"It was more like a family road trip with a rodeo built in. We had a pretty good time, though. When we were making our way back from San-tone," he smiled at his pronunciation, "we stopped at Abilene for the night. Ginger remembered seeing an advertisement for Hardin-Simmons University and asked if we could tour it. I had it in my head she was going to Hillsdale College, but she wanted a seminary degree. And the school is Baptist, which is what she wanted."

"What about Baylor? That's a Baptist school."

"We looked at it too. But Baylor was too big for her. Baylor enrolls more students than the entire population of Coeur d'Alene. I think it scared her to go someplace with so many people. Hardin-Simmons enrolls right about three thousand students and was less intimidating to her."

"So, that's how she ended up in a small school in Texas?"

"I can't believe how much time has passed. She'll graduate this fall with her bachelor's degree. Seems like yesterday I met with you and the Lair, but that was almost ten years ago." He sipped his tea. "You know? It almost killed us to see Ginger go to college."

"No doubt." He sipped his tea again. "Yes, it seems Ginger made a great choice for a school. Not every kid is intended for Ivy League Schools. Besides, doesn't she want to be in the ministry?"

"She wants to be a missionary in South America. In fact, rumor has it she is going to get married."

"Great," Gerald was pleased. "I didn't know she was engaged."

"It's nothing official, yet. Her boyfriend is super traditional and wants to talk to me first. He seems like a good kid."

"Have you checked him out yet?"

"Are you kidding me? It was the first thing I did. And he's clean. He's on a scholarship from the Southern Baptist Convention and is earmarked for a position in Paraguay when he graduates."

"Is that where Ginger's interest in South America came from?"

"Well, they met at a church function where a Wycliffe Bible translator was a guest speaker. They discovered they both had the same ideas about being full-time missionaries. A few pizzas later and they're falling in love." Justin frowned. "And now they'll be married and move off to Timbuktu or some such place. It all happened so fast."

"It does, indeed."

Connie came out of the house with a platter of sausage, cheese, and crackers, and even had decorated the plate with various pickles. Gerald was delighted to share the sausage with them and enjoyed it greatly. "That is very good pickled okra, Connie. Is it homemade?"

"Yes, it is. I make it here."

"Oh, it's not only homemade, but it's made by your own hands? Truly remarkable," he said with a wink.

"Thank you. That's also a Texas recipe. We learned how to make pickled okra from an old couple who had a fruit stand somewhere near Brady. We stopped for some watermelons and ended up with pecan pies, jerky, fresh peaches, and pickled okra. She was kind enough to tell me how to make them myself. And those watermelons! They were yellow-meat watermelons. I had never heard of them before, but they were probably the best I've ever tasted. And they were huge."

"Everything is bigger in Texas, of course." Gerald accepted another tea refill. "So, what is Kevin going to do now that his enlistment is almost over?"

"Boise State University North is practically begging him to attend their school. We'd like to see him come home, so I've been encouraging him to think about it. If he attended BSUN, it would certainly be a feather in their cap. I know the Bass Pro Shop wants him to come back and be the face of the gun range again. He really likes his Army job, though. And from what I can tell, he's very good at it."

"I'm an Army man myself," Gerald bragged. "I was drafted right out of college and spent several years flying helicopters with the 7th Cavalry. I understand how some people are so good at what they do and they should be allowed to do it. But military life comes with a sacrifice. It's very hard to have a family and be in Special Forces. And snipers are always on call. College isn't the path for everyone, but if college isn't your path, you certainly need to be on a path that will take you somewhere."

Justin nodded. "He's a good kid, and we're proud of him no matter what path he chooses."

"No, Justin, he's a good *man*," Connie said reluctantly. "It's hard to remember when it's your baby who's grown up."

Gerald nodded. "Besides our relationship with God, family is all we have that's eternal."

Justin cleared his throat. "That's actually why we invited you to come and visit. We wanted to thank you for everything you've done for us."

Gerald lifted a hand innocently. "You've done it all. I just motivated you."

Justin shook his head in disagreement. "That's not true. If you hadn't taken the time to challenge me to be a better man and a better husband, then who knows what might have happened in our lives? One thing I know, and I know this well. Marrying Connie was the best choice I've ever made. Every day hasn't been perfect, but we were always happy. And we've always been in love. Our children gave our lives meaning and purpose and we're eternally thankful for what God's given us. But you, Gerald, gave us a glimpse of what I might have lost if I took what God gave me for granted.

"Christians don't engage Christians much anymore. We're all so busy making a living and running our kids around we fail to connect with each other. We neglect our mutual responsibilities to the larger

221

body and we don't even notice we're flying solo. And we're wrong for doing so. We all wander off the path on occasion and journey from the sunlight into the shadows and it takes courage to point that out to others, lest we offend them. But in the offense there is love. And in love there is forgiveness. And in forgiveness there is healing. And in healing there is peace. But first there must be pain, and that's the uncomfortable part; it's the part we don't want to inflict on our brothers.

"When I think of it, I imagine we're all infected with a disease, but there is a cure in the form of an injection. An injection only works if it actually pierces the skin. But, we fear the needle and find it offensive. Yet, the injection won't work if you pour the medicine on the skin. The needle has to actually penetrate and cause pain. Or fear. Either way, you have to be injected to be cured.

"You showed me where I was weak and where I was wrong. You showed me my sin. And I'm thankful you chose an uncomfortable path and allowed me the opportunity to get back on track. You invested into my life and you invested in my family. There is no way to know what my secret sins might have done to my family and me, but I am thankful you intervened.

"So, I wanted to tell you I'm now going to invest in someone's life, just as you did for me. We like to use the phrase, pay it forward. Well, we're going to do the same thing. After all, to whom much is given, much is required.

"We wanted to get you a token of our appreciation." He nodded at Connie, who was suddenly holding a small gift bag. "Please take this gift and know you're a highly valued member of our family."

Gerald graciously accepted the gift and opened the bag. He carefully examined the gift and wiped a tear from his eye. He was holding a framed photograph of the Greys. The engraving on the

frame read, "To Gerald, our father. One man can make a difference."
On the bottom of the frame, the engraving read, "One choice a future
makes. Thanks for choosing us."

CHAPTER TWENTY-FOUR
Flip

Connie was furious. She was beyond furious. *In my entire lifetime, I've made love to two men only and one of them gives me an STD. Why didn't I say no to him? Why did I go down this path? Why did I push away all the people who tried to help me in the early days of the pain? Pride—that's why.* Pride and shame were the two motivating factors that drove her into isolation and caused her to abandon her own kids. And they caused her to abandon her standards.

If she didn't have shame then, well, she certainly did now. She had a sexually transmitted disease, and she could hardly bear to say the word, herpes. Truly, her monogamous marriage had protected her from so much pain.

The doctor's office told her the condition was incurable, that one in six people between the ages of fourteen and forty-nine have the virus, and ninety percent of those have no idea they're infected. The stats kept running through her mind. One in nine sexually active men are infected, but one in five active women have it.

I can't believe this is happening to me. I would have been better off to say no. Ugh, now what? If Ben gave me one STD, is he infected with something else too?

She didn't want to face Ben, and she didn't want to go home. Ginger wasn't answering her phone, as she and Mona were off worshiping some horned god in the woods. Kevin would be no source of comfort for her so she wouldn't consider involving him. She needed to clear her mind, so she started driving and went wherever her car wanted to go. She turned onto Ash Street and somehow ended up at the cemetery. *Why did I come here? I may end up here, but not today. I may be in pain, but I'm not going to give up yet.*

She turned around and drove along Cow Creek and found herself at a vista on Katka Mountain. She pulled off the road and sat in her car. *What am I going to do? I really hate living with Ben. I hate how he makes me feel like I'm always wrong and he's always right. He treats me like a dog, but where else can I go. I have no options. And I can't keep continually forgiving him—that's wrong too. All I'm doing is enabling him to be a jerk. I've got to find help.*

Her own ultra-religious family had disowned her for getting a divorce and even blamed her for Justin's infidelity. *How could they blame me? How just was that?* She hardly ever spoke to her family, and they practically disowned Kevin once he started spending short spans in the county jail. They fully disowned Ginger for abandoning her faith, much less for marrying a woman. But when they continued to blame Connie for Justin's affair, she walked away from them. She had enough pain in her life without being hammered by people who were so religious they were harsh and critical. What good was that? If that was Christianity, then she wanted nothing to do with it either.

But, she knew that wasn't Christianity. It was a distortion of Christianity. True Christianity was about setting people free from bondage, and receiving forgiveness for sinful behavior. It was about freedom and life.

As she drove up the mountain, she saw the Katka overlook and decided she needed fresh air. She got out of her car and stood along the guardrail along the overlook. The forest spread out like a fan below her, cascading along the edge of the mountain and forming a wall along the fields surrounding the Kootenai River below. The fields were bright yellow and green, making the landscape look as if primary colors were the only colors God chose to work with. She could see Bonners Ferry scattered along the ridges above the river, and Moyie Springs off the right with its signature sawmill and the river bridge. The majestic mountains were beyond the river valley, stretching out in every direction as far as the eyes could see; their peaks were still snow-covered and inviting. She could smell the fresh air, enhanced with the scent of pine and wildflowers. What a beautiful day!

For a moment, she felt peace. She wanted to cry out to God in a loud voice, but she whispered to Him, "Please forgive me." That was all she could summon for the moment, but she certainly felt God's warmth in her heart. God never made it complicated. He gave simple answers.

She'd made such a mess of her life. And the lives of her children too. She made so many selfish, childish decisions, and she feared the consequences would be more than she could bear. *I have to get out of this really bad situation. I need to end my relationship with Ben and I need to find a place to live. Kevin can help me if I can find him. He's probably at Chet's house. That's where he always is.*

She grabbed her cell phone and dialed his number. "Hi, Kevin. Please call me when you get this message. I'm moving out of Ben's house and I would like for you to come help me if you will. Thanks, babe. I love you, Mom."

Where am I going to spend the night? Oh, I don't care—I'll just grab some things and leave. Ben can jump into the lake for all I care. To think I thought he was my savior—he sure doesn't fit that bill. Never mind.

Maybe I can get home before he gets off work. Then I can get in and out without him noticing.

Connie was eternally grateful when she arrived at his home and saw Ben's pickup was gone. She dashed into the house and hurriedly tossed clothes and toiletries into a bag. *What else do I need? That's it. I can come back for the rest after he's gone for the day. Oh, can't forget my pillow.* She glanced at the bed. Horrible memories flooded over her of all the times he practically forced her to lay with him. *Those days are over!*

She closed the bedroom door behind her and stepped around the corner. Ben was there.

"Where are you going?" he demanded.

"I'm leaving, Ben."

"Says who?"

"Please don't make this hard. I can't be here anymore."

His eyes narrowed and his nostrils were flaring. "What brought this on?"

She couldn't get into this right now. "Please, just let me leave. We can talk later if you like."

"Later? What's wrong with now? Don't I deserve an explanation? After all, I opened my home to you and I shared my bed with you. You owe me an explanation."

"Fine. Whatever," she said dismissively. "You gave me herpes. I'm leaving. And that's all."

"Herpes?" he roared. "You have an STD? Where did you get it?"

"From you."

"Wrong! You've been sleeping around. Is that why you're so hot to leave? Is your boyfriend waiting for you in the car?" He turned and looked out the open door. "Who is he?"

"There's no boyfriend, Ben. And you're the only man I've been with, so you better get yourself checked out for an STD."

"How dare you? How dare you bring that disease into my home? How long have you been cheating on me? TELL ME!"

She lifted a hand to calm him. "Easy, Ben. There is no cheating. There are no boyfriends. I just can't stay here anymore." He was standing between her and the open door, and he showed no signs of surrender.

"You can't leave until you tell me who it is. I want to know who needs killin'."

"Ben, you know better. You're it. There's no one else."

"Then why leave?"

A car door slammed behind him. "Ah, so your boyfriend is coming." He spun around and saw Kevin making his way up the steps; he looked angry. "What do you want, boy?"

"Get out of the way, Ben," he snarled.

"Kevin?" Connie called out. "Everything is okay. I'm just leaving."

"You're not going anywhere until we settle this," Ben said over his shoulder. He wasn't taking his eyes off Kevin.

"Mom? Just step around him and come outside."

Connie tried to get outside; she pressed her way to the door and tried to squeeze around him, but he steadied himself and blocked the door. "Ben, don't do this. We don't want trouble. Just let me leave."

"You think you can just use me and then leave whenever you're done? I don't think so."

"Fine, I'm calling the cops." She grabbed her cell phone and started pressing numbers.

His anger flashed and he spun around, slapping the phone from her hand. It landed against the wall and the battery cover flipped off. Kevin saw him slap her, so he lowered his head and executed a full body tackle, driving Ben from the door frame, collapsing with him on the floor.

Ben was already insane with anger; he threw Kevin off his back and tried to roll over, but Kevin was a scrapper, and he wasn't going to stop. He lifted his fist to punch Ben, but Ben rolled over and scrambled to his feet. Connie was yelling hysterically at both men, trying to bring order to the situation, but the fight descended into chaos. They began scrambling for weapons and were throwing lamps and chairs at each other, landing punches and evading kicks.

Connie tried to get between them. Ben was already swinging a full roundhouse punch at Kevin—she walked right into it. His fist landed with so much force her teeth snapped and her nose collapsed. Her head rolled back, she landed face first on a broken chair and lay motionless. Kevin saw the punch and his anger soared to rage. He began executing kicks and punches Ben had no ability to defend against and systematically beat Ben until he collapsed in a heap at the door to the kitchen.

Kevin turned to Connie, "Mom?" He rushed to her aid, but she didn't respond. She'd been knocked out cold by the punch; when she landed on the broken chair legs, one punctured her chest. Kevin had no idea she was injured and rolled her over on her back. When he did, the shaft of wood sticking from her chest startled him, and he reached and pulled it out without stopping to think. Blood immediately began to spurt from the wound, landing several feet away. "Oh, no," he mumbled. What was he supposed to do? He wanted to jam the wood back into the hole, but he didn't think that was the right thing to do. He grabbed his phone and dialed 911. "Please come quick," he pleaded. "My mom is injured and is bleeding like crazy. Her boyfriend attacked her and now she's hurt really bad. Come quick!"

"Where are you calling from, sir?"

"We're at …" he heard movement behind him, but before he could react, Ben jammed a butcher knife into his back. A searing pain tore through him and he lost the function of his left arm. He dropped the phone and tried to speak, but his lips weren't working. He still held the shaft of wood in his right hand. He spun around and jammed the jagged spear deep into Ben's throat. Ben immediately grabbed for the spike, but he was bleeding hard, and his breathing was cut off. He desperately clawed at the spike, but he couldn't pull it out. His lungs were filling with blood quickly and a horrible, gurgling sound erupted from his chest. Within seconds, he passed out never to take another breath.

The knife was still firmly jammed into Kevin's back and he could taste the blood he was starting to cough up. *What's up with Mom?* He stumbled to Connie and looked down at her. Her face was smashed and smeared and she didn't look like a woman at all. The blood spurting from her chest was barely oozing now. She had bled out in less than a minute. "Oh … Mom …" he managed to say from frothy lips—his last words before he collapsed on top of her.

Ginger and Mona were on a weeklong backpacking trip and had no contact with the rest of the world. The authorities had no idea where they were or how to reach them, so the girls were blissfully unaware Connie and Kevin were murder victims, and that Ben died in the struggle. Kevin survived until the police came, but he died before the ambulance arrived. In the ensuing investigation, three additional murder victims were discovered buried in Ben's backyard. The truth was now revealed his wife, Sandy Simpson, didn't move to Seattle to live with her mom; she never left home.

The impact of the losses affected Ginger deeply, and she had to be hospitalized for severe depression. She was unable to attend the funerals and was placed on suicide watch for the week that followed them. As time progressed, she didn't improve and Mona was forced to have her committed to a psychiatric hospital for treatment. She spent much of her time trying to commune with the god and goddess, pleading for their relief, but they were unable to help her. During that time, she drifted further and further from sanity, and eventually became totally insane. The remainder of her days was lost to her, and she began eternity long before dying.

Flip, who had already dismissed most of his emotional connections with his family, seemed to absorb the loss without much difficulty. As he was the surviving family member, he arranged for both funerals and returned to North Dakota, vowing to never return to Bonners Ferry.

Connie's family refused to attend the funerals, as they believed the deaths were a testimony to the depravity of Connie's sin, and they continued to blame her for destroying her family. Only briefly did they make contact with Flip, at which time they apologized for Connie's behavior. He was gracious and told them he had forgiven her long ago and he only looked upon the past with fond memories. Even Flip wouldn't talk ill of the dead while attending their funeral.

He stopped by the hospital to say goodbye to Ginger. He introduced her to Erica, the new love of his life—new as she was divorced from her jailbird husband and now fully committed to Flip. They were very happy together. Ginger was either unable to respond to them or unwilling; they weren't sure which it was. Either way, she failed to bless her father in his efforts to seek happiness.

Even though he and Erica didn't stay together in the years that followed, and despite the fact that he bounced from one failed relationship to the next and one continually lesser job to the next, Flip continued to maintain that he was happy.

CHAPTER TWENTY-FIVE
Justin

At the 63rd Annual Hilton Head Bank and Market Conference, Justin took center stage on the opening night and graciously waited for the applause to subside. He lifted a hand to the crowd and waved to them, deeply appreciating their enthusiasm to see him.

"My dear friends, ten years ago today, I stood before you an ordinary man. I was a very simple man who was a husband, father, and banker. But I soon realized I was only as ordinary as I chose to be when Gerald Alexander approached me and gave me a push to find my potential. He held me accountable for my choices and offered me the opportunity to be a better man. I'm not ashamed to tell you that ten years ago I was a different man. I was a half-hearted husband and father and my priorities were out of balance. With the guidance of a great mentor, I realigned my life and surrendered my future to my Heavenly Father. Another contributing factor was the influence New Life Ministries and the book, *Every Man's Battle,* had in my life. If you struggle with sexual integrity issues, I highly recommend these resources to you.

"Not far from this location, I stood on the beach and was offered the opportunity of a lifetime. I had to choose to be faithful to my wife and children and my God and faith or choose to seek temporary pleasure in the affections of another woman's arms. I'm ashamed to say I wavered for just a moment before choosing the path that would bring me life. I cannot imagine what my life would have been had I chosen differently. Only God can foresee such things. I'm reminded of the classic movie starring Jimmy Stewart, *It's a Wonderful Life.* In that film, George Bailey gets to see what his life would have been like had he never been born. Well, none of us knows exactly how different the world would be, in that case, but I do know this: no man is an island unto himself. Every decision we make impacts multiple people for either good or bad. This may be why God commands us to guard against idle words and actions. Our family motto has become, *One choice a future makes.*

"The years have come and gone for me and my family. We've weathered every storm with as much grace and dignity as we could muster. We've shared both bad times and good times, but our good times have significantly outnumbered the bad. Because of God's blessings in our lives, we have continued to prosper. This year, *Time Magazine* named me one of the top one hundred businessmen of the year ..." he waited until the applause settled before continuing. "They did a full article on my vision to see Eagle Summit when everyone else saw only an intersection of Highway 95 and Highway 2. The proceeds of my business enterprise are not my own. I seek to find ways to reinvest money into our community and help advance the Kingdom. Earlier this year, I was honored to fly to Stockholm, Sweden, where I was given the Nobel Memorial Prize in Economic Sciences. I'm grateful God has seen fit to bless me so. But that is enough about me.

"Connie's investment with her battered women's ministry continues to produce great results. She first funded a home in Bonners Ferry so women had a place to go if they needed to escape from their situation at home. She has now established a safe house in every neighboring community to help rescue battered and abused families. She established scholarships for any woman who would make the effort to attend classes at Boise State University North, or any other school. For many, it meant the difference between returning to an abusive husband or starting a new life. In addition to her work with battered women, she authored the best-selling novel, *Love's Determined Grace*, which was loosely inspired by her ministry.

"Together we have mentored several different married couples to pay forward what Gerald gave us ten years ago. While each of them is in a completely different situation from my own family, we are helping to stabilize America one family at a time.

"God has opened many doors I never imagined possible. I've served as a consultant to every presidential administration since then and I've repeatedly turned down the opportunity to seek public office in almost every capacity possible. I feel I have more influence to make a positive change from my current place in life and that being a senator or representative would only hinder my ability to influence politics.

"Our daughter, Ginger, married her college sweetheart shortly after graduation from Hardin-Simmons and they began working with the Southern Baptist Convention in Paraguay, helping to establish the Kingdom of God there. She seems to have a knack working with people who follow pagan ideologies. They have prospered greatly in their ministry—many generations will be changed because of the efforts Ginger and her family have made. She's provided us five grandchildren. They've kept the airways busy flying back and forth between South America and wherever we happened to be at the time. Since my grandkids are so adorable, I highly recommend you buy stock in the airline industry, as I intend to keep the airways busy in the years to come.

"Many of you have asked about our son, Kevin. He returned to Bonners Ferry for a brief time once his initial enlistment was fulfilled. He attended BSUN for four years. He loved his work in the Army and didn't want to leave military service, so he decided to join the Army National Guard. Even though Bonners Ferry has a Guard unit, he joined the 19th Special Forces Group, which is headquartered in Draper, Utah. He was able to secure a position with A Company, 1st Battalion/19th SFG, a detachment in Fort Lewis, Washington, which is outside of Seattle. He chose the 19th because they're one of two Special Forces groups in the National Guard and because he could continue to operate as a sniper and maintain his Airborne status.

"While he was attending BSUN, he met and married a woman who is very similar to Connie. The two of them are happy—well, as happy as an Army couple can be," he added with a wry smile. "They've endured many difficult deployments over the years, but they've made it work and managed to raise two wonderful kids in the process. After Kevin had graduated from BSUN, he accepted a commission as an officer. His skills and reputation have made him a legend.

"I don't know what might have been had I not chosen to walk in righteousness. I'm certain by my choice I set in motion many things that I have no ability to calculate. But I do know many people's lives have been changed as a result of one decision to be faithful to my wife so many years ago.

"Truly, once choice a future makes."

Travis writes:

This was almost my story. Something like this happened to me. I was faced with making the same decision Justin had to make. A few years ago in our all too recent history, my family suddenly found itself in a death grip that could have devastated our lives. The problem was me.

I was a Christian of more than three decades. I am an ordained minister and I have years of practical ministry experience. In short, I was not the type of person one would expect to cheat on his wife. At the time of the incident, which was only a few weeks long in its entirety, Sarah and I had been married for almost ten years. As is true with all marriages, we had good years and bad years. This happened during a good year.

We were probably doing the best we had ever done—despite all our concerns, we were committed to each other for life. We were going to have another baby and I was just about to start a new career with great potential. *Then it happened.*

I was required to travel for five months to complete some mandatory training for my job. So, I left my family in Texas and flew to the East Coast, where I lived for the next twenty weeks. During that time, I saw my family once. During that time, I met another woman.

She was an attractive woman. She had a warm smile and was a pleasant person. When I met her, I felt no special attraction toward her. In fact, I hardly noticed her beyond all the other pretty women at the mall. She was only one of many faces in a crowded mall food court. I simply bought a coke from her and went on my way. The next time I saw her I bought a coke and went on my way. This happened for several weekends in a row. Before long, we were chatting much as daily acquaintances would. Then one day, I mentioned I needed to call a cab to take me across town—she offered to give me a ride. There was no flirting or manipulation. She was a nice woman who simply offered to help. I don't believe either of us had any intentions of getting involved with each other at all. She told me she was married but that they were permanently separated and waiting for a divorce. She was a Christian woman and had a genuine relationship with God. I never perceived any threat in my seemingly innocent relationship with her.

I was enticed to spend more time with her, and it happened so slowly I never saw it coming. Before long, I was attracted to this woman. And I had to make a decision. I struggled with what to do. And I struggled with it longer than I should have. I tried to convince myself the relationship was one God wanted, but we both knew that wasn't true. Had it not been for my wife, who challenged me to tell her what was going on, I would have fallen—and I would have lost everything. My wife refused to allow our family to fall apart. Looking back, I feel great relief God was merciful to my family, and me, and that no permanent harm was done. We experienced a "bullet burn" so to speak.

I could have followed a different path. I could be Flip, just as easily as I could be Justin. One resource that helped me tremendously was a book titled, *Every Man's Battle*. Get it. Get it now!

I know I'm not alone. I know many of you would/could share

a similar story. Let us covenant now to be better men and women, who follow God's path and, who determine to do what is right not what feels good. Let us change the world and let it begin with me. Remember,

One choice a future makes.

Discussion Points

1. What did Connie and Justin's life look like before the conference?

2. How might each of them have handled the phone call better?

3. Given that Justin was vulnerable, was Gerald right to test Justin? Did he have the right to test him with such tactics? What are the moral implications involved?

4. Would Gerald have approached Justin with his legacy had Justin not had secret sins in his life? Were the secret sins the things that made Justin a viable heir to the legacy?

5. What did Gerald see in Justin that made him confident in the outcome of his test?

6. Why did Flip fall to temptation when Justin didn't? Is it true to suggest Flip was always tucked away inside of Justin?

7. How could Connie have helped prevent Justin's private struggle? How would he have responded to her if she tried?

8. Connie insists Justin did something wrong just allowing Dahlia to get close to him, and his considering Dahlia's temptation was a betrayal itself. Do you agree with her?

9. Did Justin's perception of Connie change after he passed the test?

10. Why did Justin convince himself Mercedes was the best choice for an assistant? Is it unreasonable that he was willing to allow her beauty to help motivate his clients?

11. At what point did Flip actually fall? Was his sin against God, Connie, or himself?

12. How vulnerable are we to our secret sins? Would most men have fallen into Dahlia's trap?

13. Did it help or hinder Justin knowing that Gerald was going to hold him accountable for everything he did? How would you react if Gerald were holding you accountable in such fashion?

14. Who is the God-like figure in the story? Who is the Satan-like figure? Are both elements necessary to tell Justin's story?

15. How does shame factor into both storylines and how did it control the characters?

16. Justin chose to invest his wealth in the entertainment industry. What are your reactions to his decision? If you were given the opportunity to speculatively invest such wealth, how would your path be different from Justin's?

17. Why was Flip so determined to leave Connie and his life behind?

18. Why did Flip rationalize that he and Connie didn't love each other anymore or that they weren't happy?

19. Is it probable that Connie would have allowed herself to fall victim to Ben? Was she vulnerable to him, or was he merely an escape plan for her?

20. Flip's reality was unpleasant. Who was the biggest victim of his choices?

21. Do you believe that one choice can alter the course of your life, or is your future already determined?

22. Is it possible there is another reality running parallel to your life where you have made similar decisions that altered the natural course of your life?